THE CLADIE BAILEY STORY

by WENDELL TROGDON

BACKROADS PRESS

✓

Distributed by Wendell Trogdon
and Backroads Press
P.O. Box 651
Mooresville, IN 46158

ISBN 0-964-2371-0-5

Cover by Gary Varvel

Printed by Country Pines Printing
Shoals, Indiana

ABOUT THE AUTHOR

Chances are no one is better qualified to tell the Cladie Bailey story than Wendell Trogdon.

Trogdon is the author of ten other books, four of them about life in southern Indiana at the time Cladie Bailey was a young adult. The author also has written five books about basketball, Indiana's game, which Cladie Bailey coached.

Trogdon grew up less than two miles from Bailey's southern Indiana home, went to the same church and school Bailey once attended and observed him as a teacher and as a basketball coach.

The author used his 40 years experience as a reporter and newspaper editor to research and write "Out Front, The Cladie Bailey Story."

OUT FRONT
The Cladie Bailey Story

Only the young die in battle, many as heroes of wars they seek to finish in the defense of freedom. Most are soon forgotten, except by their families, their deeds of bravery and valor stored in dust-coated archives. They deserve better. This is a memorial to one of those men.

CONTENTS

ACKNOWLEDGMENTS

Two men who are not named in this book helped make it possible. Morris Adams of Indianapolis was a member of Cladie Bailey's Company G when it was sent overseas to Australia. He provided information and background which was the impetus needed to start our research. Elbert Watson of Carmel, Ind., mentioned our plans for a book in the World War II Times he edits. That item led a number of Bailey's fellow officers to contact us with information.

Our gratitude goes to those officers and men and to others who shared their memories of, and affection for Cladie Bailey.

This book is not meant to be a definitive description of the battles in which the 126th Infantry Regiment was engaged. It is, however, a look at the involvement of one of its officers, a man remembered a half-century later for his friendship, his leadership, his character and his bravery.

A PERSONAL GLIMPSE

Cladie Bailey was almost a generation older than I, a man of 30 when I was a boy of 11.

His parents lived two miles from our farm, a neighbor on the road to Heltonville, a tiny southern Indiana town in the hills of northeastern Lawrence County. His grandfather, James "Toll" Bailey, was my grandmother Elizabeth's brother.

My first memory of Cladie was on the diamond where he played independent baseball on those long, hot summer Sundays in the late 1930s. Later, as a fifth and sixth grader, I watched as he coached the Heltonville High School basketball teams in the 1939-40 and 1940-41 season. And like most students, I knew we had lost a teacher and a friend when he was called to active duty with the U.S. Army in April, 1941. School would not be the same in the years ahead.

I would not see him again. But as he had others, he had unknowingly influenced my life and I would not forget him.

Wendell Trogdon

PART I

CHAPTER I

Seasons of Change

A hot August sun blistered the galvanized roof, turning the inside of the barn into an oven without ventilation.

If the southern Indiana heat bothered the man down in the silo pit, he didn't complain. There was more digging and shoveling to do and it would not get done if he stopped often to wipe his brow and rest.

Instead he let the perspiration filter down his short sideburns, past his wrinkle-free profile, soaking the blue denim shirt, letting it cling to a granite-like body and accentuate his muscular frame.

He swung a mattock deep into the red clay time after time, then reached for a long handle shovel and tossed out the loosened dirt where Wes and his sons, Wayne and Wendell, loaded it onto a gravel bed on a horse-drawn wagon.

In a couple of weeks, the corn would be ready to be turned to silage, so the work crew was facing a deadline. The pit had to be finished and the used silo Wes had bought would need to be erected over the pit in the corner of the barn.

Wes emptied the load in a gully washed into the side of a hill, pulling out the worn three-by-three-inch timbers at the bottom of the gravel bed, letting the dirt fall free.

He made a detour as he returned to the barn, stopping at the shed-covered spring to pick up a giant watermelon, chilled by water that flowed cold and clean from a vein in the hill into a reservoir basin.

Wes returned to the barn, laid the watermelon on a mound of hay and said to the man in the pit, "Time for a break, Clade."

"Clade" was Cladie Bailey, college-educated, a bachelor who at 30 had seen life's sunshine as well as its darkness. By that summer of 1940, he had survived economic hardship, had been idled by the Great Depression. Brighter days, it appeared, were ahead.

He would return in a few weeks to school at Heltonville, a southern Indiana hamlet where he was a teacher and coach. Wes paid him $2 a day for his labor. It wasn't much, but times were still hard. And Clade, a man who had washed dishes in order to attend college, could stretch a few dollars a long way. He wouldn't receive his first check from Jack Clark, the Pleasant Run Township trustee who ran the school system, until two weeks after school started.

And Bailey, even though he did not know it at the time, would in a few days, meet the girl he would later marry. Some of the money might be used to take her to the movies at the Von Ritz and Indiana theaters in Bedford.

Wes stuck his big Barlow pocket knife into the watermelon, and it burst open, exposing a red heart, moist and inviting. He handed "Clade" the first piece, a thick slab, for hired hands were considered guests and served first on farms.

Cladie bit into the big slice, held it in his mouth to savor the taste, appreciate the sweet coolness against his parched throat.

Wes' sons watched, for Cladie like their dad, was a man to be copied, an example to be followed. They felt privileged to sit there, listening to the conversation.

Wayne would be a seventh grader in the fall. He knew Cladie would coach the junior high team, as well as the varsity and second team, for he had no assistants. Wendell would be in the sixth grade, but he, too, looked forward to later playing for "Clade" or "Mr. Bailey" as he would have to call him when school started.

The break lasted no more than 20 minutes, but the four of them had devoured most of the watermelon, littering the pit with seeds. Cladie jumped back into the hole to toss out the seeds amid the loosened dirt.

In another day or two the pit was finished, bottomed out against the solid rock. Wes "settled up" with Cladie, writing a check with a stubby indelible pencil he pulled from the bib pocket of his overalls.

"Don't pay any attention if any one bad mouths Clade. He's a good man," Wes said to his sons as Bailey drove off up the gravel road to Ind. 58 and west toward Heltonville.

The silo was erected, tongue-and-groove sides fitted in place, and filled with silage. School started again, seasons went through their full cycle, and another summer arrived. The seeds of the watermelon sprouted and the vines covered the area where the dirt from the silo pit had been dumped.

Wes could no longer ask Cladie to help if he needed a hired hand. Cladie was in Louisiana, an Army lieutenant preparing for war. The world was changing fast and even a farmer and his two sons could sense the gathering of war clouds they could not yet see.

The spreading watermelon vines, however, let them remember Cladie and that August of 1940.

CHAPTER II

A Time of Transition

Cladie Bailey was born in a time of transition and he would never escape the inevitability of change.

The date was October 26, 1910, the sixth anniversary of his parents' wedding. It was a time when babies were delivered by doctors who arrived at rural homes on horseback. Cladie was the fourth child of James and Mamie Ann Meadows Bailey, who had been married in 1904. Their other children at the time were Doris, who was almost five; Justice, who was three, and James, who had just turned two.

A hint of fall was in the air that Wednesday. Clouds shaded the sun as the day lengthened and the afternoon Bedford Daily Mail warned that the night would be much colder and forecast a killing frost for the weekend.

It was time for a fire to be built in the wood stove in the frame house.

If father Jim had a chance to scan the newspaper as he sat by the fire and the kerosene lamp, he would have read about President William Howard Taft and other developments of the day. But it would have been the ads that told him more about the economy and the era in which Cladie was born.

A Page One story recapped the 1910 World Series, explained that each of the 23 members of the Philadelphia Athletics would receive a $2,062.74 share for winning the championship.

Neither Jim nor Mamie would realize at the time the role baseball would play in the life of their new born.

A classified advertisement from the Globe Store in Bedford boasted, "We're selling the best shirt for $1 that ever sold for that price." Other ads offered "Sewing Machines $20 to $45" and "pianos and player pianos $200 and up."

A big advertisement for a Maxwell, "the economy car," gave an indication of the changes that would come in the 20th Century. The auto, with spoke wheels, running board, brake levers and canvas top, was pictured among a sales pitch: "Automobile vs. Horse. A public test of the Maxwell Car and a horse and buggy on the streets of New York and its suburbs under actual conditions of traffic, has just been completed. The Maxwell per passenger mile, 1.8 cents. Horse and buggy, passenger mile, 2.5 cents."

It was an ad meant to attract readers in Bedford and Mitchell and other towns with paved streets. Roads around Jim's place weren't yet ready to handle horseless carriages.

Besides, folks like Jim already had horses and buggies but not $900 for the four cylinder, 22 horsepower Maxwell Model Q-11.

Life went on, much as it had before Cladie arrived. Brother Veralin William, who would be called Bill, was born two years later in 1912. But two years after that, an older brother, Justice, died at the age of seven and was buried in Mundell Cemetery outside the church the family attended.

Brother Jesse Paul was born in 1915, sister, Helen Mary, in 1917. The family was complete.

* * *

On a map, the Fullen school, a one-room building attended by students in grades 1 through 6, didn't appear to be far from the Bailey home. It wasn't an easy walk, however.

Leatherwood Creek, a stream that began a couple of miles to the east, was across what is now Ind. 58 from the Bailey home. In the fall it was usually dry, its soapstone bottom smooth. Rains, however could turn it into a flooded arroyo of chocolate-like water that flowed swift and deep. It was an obstacle the Bailey children faced a number of times each school year.

Eventually their dad, a carpenter, would build a bridge for them to cross.

A trail worn by a daily march led along the creek before winding up a steep hill where the terrain leveled out as it went past an old graveyard a few hundred feet north of the school. It was a trip that was made day after day, Mondays through Fridays, for eight months each year.

Little did Cladie know at the time that it would be the start of an education that would lead him to Indiana University . . . and indirectly to destiny in the South Pacific.

* * *

Electricity had not reached rural areas around Heltonville, wouldn't until after World War II. Radio didn't become a household item until the late 1920s. Movies were silent. Horses and buggies were more common than cars like the Maxwell.

Except for an occasional trip to towns such as Zelma, Norman and Heltonville, social activity was limited to visits with neighbors and church activities. It was at Mundell Christian Church where Cladie and others his age made their first friends outside the family.

Meals were cooked over a wood range. Bread was baked from flour milled from home-grown wheat. Potatoes were grown in the garden and stored in a bin in a cellar, which was ringed with shelves that held hundreds of jars of fruits and vegetables canned in the summer.

Farm homes had no central heat and warm blankets kept lads like Cladie Bailey warm as they nestled on feather ticks or straw mattresses.

It was a world limited by geography, but not by imagination. A boy, without television or video games, had time to read books, leaf through magazines, let his mind roam free. He could learn from listening to his father and other men, men born in another century to parents who had come to Lawrence County through the Appalachians from the Carolinas and Georgia.

A boy could use maps to view the world as it was in those World War I years and beyond. He could find Serbia, where that war had started, locate what "over" meant when soldiers sang "We're Going Over . . ."

The South Pacific wasn't in the news much in those years, but young Cladie Bailey may have spotted Australia, Papua New Guinea and the Philippine Islands on a map in a book. He could not have imagined that he would some day play a part in the history of each.

CHAPTER III

An Athlete in Action

Cladie's walks to school were not over when his years at Fullen ended. There was no bus transportation to Heltonville, a 2.7-mile walk from his door to the school, would be none for two years until Fullen School closed.

At that time, Cladie, Bill and Jesse rode a bus, called a hack in those days, to Heltonville. The bus was driven by Ed Bailey, an uncle who lived nearby on Ind. 58 which by then had been paved.

* * *

It was a time when basketball was becoming popular as a high school sport, more so even than baseball. Games became community events, drawing fans eager for excitement on Friday nights after a week's work.

Some men are born with athletic ability and Cladie Bailey was one of them. His hand-eye coordination let him learn to play most sports quickly, naturally, a gift that would serve him well for the next 14 years.

He was a high school varsity player as a freshman in the 1924-25 season, the year the first gymnasium was built at Heltonville, the year a 4,500 seat basketball palace was erected at Bedford. He became a standout as a sophomore a year later when he played with Glenard Scott, Estel Hawkins, Elmer Etter, George East, Herman Mitchell, Walter "Dutch" Holt, Norton Tanksley, Arthur Ford and Howard Todd on the 1925-26 team.

Expectations for success grew among the Heltonville fans as the 1926 sectional at Bedford approached. The team drew Tunnelton to open the sectional. A victory would match the "Julianmen," as the Bedford papers called the Heltonville team, against the winner of the West Baden-Oolitic game.

Coach Ray Julian's players warmed up for the Tunnelton game amidst the fanfare of the opening game, moving a bit quicker in their drills, keeping attuned to the Bedford High School band. Before the game was a minute old, Bailey had scored a basket. He would finish with nine points, leading his team to a 31-9 victory.

Tunnelton was led by junior O. O. Dixon, who had two of his team's four baskets. It was a continuation of a friendly rivalry and it would not be the last time the paths of Bailey and Dixon would cross.

Heltonville fell to West Baden, 26-18, in the second round of the sectional. Bailey was held to four points, but he would have two more years of competition.

* * *

Fans around Heltonville already knew about Cladie Bailey's athletic ability. They were eager for others to see his talent on display at the 1927 Bedford sectional.

On the 1926-27 team besides Bailey were Elmer Etter, another big scorer, Estel Hawkins, Ed Cain, George East, Norton Tanksley, Fred Maher, Herman Mitchell, Howard Todd and Goffria Turpen.

It was March 4 when Heltonville, led by Bailey's 10 points, defeated French Lick, 28-17, in the opening round of the sectional. Bailey scored seven points in an easier 27-13 triumph over Orleans.

West Baden then fell to Bailey's team, 28-20, in the Saturday afternoon semifinal. Midway through the game, Bailey tipped in a miss, then dribbled through the entire West Baden team for a lay up and sank a free throw for a three-point play. It was all the momentum Heltonville needed to win. Bailey had a game-high 15 points.

It was a performance that led the Bedford Daily Times, in its "Hardwood Echoes" column, to write: "Coach Julian's Heltonville squad is to be commended for its excellent showing. He has a group of clean, hard fighting youngsters, who never give up and Bailey is outstanding. His dribbling and shooting has featured every game in which the Pleasant Run team has played.

"Coach Julian's Heltonville quintet of youthful athletes has made a gallant fight for supremacy. On three occasions during the tournament they have demonstrated their superiority over their opponents and none can justly deprive them of being the gamest of the 13 teams entered for competition here."

Kind words. But Bailey and his team would have preferred a fourth victory, the last being for the championship.

The Bedford band presented what the newspaper called "a darling spectacle" at the opening of the final game. It was given a rousing cheer of appreciation at the completion of the program, but it was the game, a battle between the big school vs. the small one that fans had come to see.

Bedford took an early lead, but Bailey hit from center court and Tanksley followed to cut the margin to 13-8 and Heltonville trailed only 13-10 at the half.

Bedford started the second half with a spurt and quickly widened the margin. It was obvious the winners had planned to stop Bailey, force him to shoot from outside. Except for one basket, from long-range, his shots did not fall. The final score was Bedford 51, Heltonville 19, but the losers had gained respect.

Again the Times commented: "It was a regrettable defeat they (Heltonville) suffered Saturday night and if local fans could have had a voice in the matter they would have qualified these youngsters for regional play along with the Iveymen (Bedford)."

Bailey and most of his teammates were juniors. They would be back to play another day.

* * *

The Heltonville team, led by Bailey, had been the surprise of the 1926-27 season. It would no longer be overlooked, no longer be underdogs, especially against county teams.

The Bedford newspapers didn't always report the outcome of the Heltonville games during the season. One story did feature a contest with Oolitic:

"One of the hardest games on the Oolitic schedule was disposed of last night when Oolitic defeated Heltonville 37 to 36. The game could have been called anyone's up until the final gun. The score was tied at 35 with 90 seconds to play.

"The Oolitic gym was crowded with one of the largest delegations from Heltonville ever to witness an Oolitic-Heltonville game. It was a big fight from start to finish."

A few days later Heltonville crushed the Bedford "Seconds" —a term used for the reserve team—39-11. The newspaper reported, "Guard Bailey, with 12 points, and Forward Ed Cain starred for the winners."

It would be another season of more victories than defeats. And again Heltonville would do well in the sectional . . . until it met the powerful Bedford team.

Led by Bailey, Heltonville edged Williams in the opening round 30-29. Williams was ahead late in the game and went into a stall to preserve its lead. The tactic backfired. Heltonville gradually chipped away at the deficit, then went ahead to stay when Bailey hit a basket and added a free throw to finish with 17 points.

Heltonville returned the next day to face West Baden. It overcame a four-point deficit in the first half to lead 10-9. With Heltonville ahead 12-11 after the break, Bailey hit a free throw, sank a shot from mid-court that hit nothing but net, then added two free throws.

West Baden couldn't recover from the one-man blitz. Bailey, according to the Times, "executed some beautiful dribbling to retain the ball until the final gun cracked." Heltonville won 22-15.

In the sectional semi-finals, Heltonville edged Shawswick, 18-17. And again Bailey was outstanding, scoring half of his team's points.

And again it would be Heltonville vs. Bedford in the finals. And it was Bailey and his underdog teammates who help draw 7,000 fans, believed to be the biggest crowd ever to see a game in the 4,500-seat gym that would be the site of sectional competition until the 1970s.

Bedford raced to a 20-2 lead and Heltonville was never able to recover. The final score was 49-11, which seems like a wide margin, until it is pointed out the Bedford team had defeated French Lick, 57-10.

The margin would be less painful in the weeks to come. Bedford continued to mow down opponents in the state tournament before reaching the final four when it lost to eventual state champion Muncie.

The Bedford Daily Mail in its Monday editions paid tribute to Bailey and his team:

"The Julianmen made a gallant fight, but because of close battles in the second round and in the semifinals, they were somewhat weary and off form. Bailey, Heltonville's star floor guard, took numerous long shots but was unable to connect except in one case."

Heltonville had been sectional runners-up two straight years, bringing a pride to the community that would last as long as there was a Heltonville High School.

Fans would point out for years to come that Bedford had eight times Heltonville's enrollment, that it had the home floor advantage. It would be a refrain heard again and again over the decades as Bedford continued to dominate its own sectionals.

On the 1927-28 team with Bailey were Ed Cain, Fred Maher, Herman Mitchell, Howard Todd, Carl Todd, Glenn Allen, Ray Turpen and Estel Hawkins.

* * *

Two months after his high school basketball career ended, Bailey graduated with seven other seniors on April 28, 1928. His diploma was signed by Randall Inman, the principal; O.O. Hall, the county school superintendent, and Jasper Cain, the Pleasant Run Township trustee who also was the town doctor.

Bailey had been more than a high school athlete. He had been a good student whose report cards, like his diploma, were saved by his mother and still remain as family treasures.

He was well-liked, popular among the other seniors, Estel Hawkins, Fred Maher, George Parish, Florence Todd, Howard Todd, Laverne Norman Todd and Goffria Turpen.

He also had friends among the underclassmen. "He was as good of a friend as I had when I was in school," Ray Turpen recalls. "He was a nice person."

Turpen remembered those days seven decades later. "Clade was one of the better players around in high school. He was usually up and at 'em . . . and always out front."

* * *

Those were the days when Cladie and brother Bill were constant companions. "He and I and Shorty White ran around together all the time," Bill recalls.

* * *

Heltonville did not have a high school baseball team in the 1920s. "Oh, we played a little baseball out on the grass some times, but we didn't play baseball as a competitive sport in school," Ray Turpen recalled.

No matter! Cladie Bailey was born, it seemed, to excel in whatever sport he chose to play. He learned baseball playing in summer games on scraped diamonds, developing pitches to fool enemy batters, earning a reputation for his savvy on the diamond.

Over the next four years, batters in collegiate ranks from Minnesota to Mississippi would return to their dugouts, shaking their heads, fooled by another Bailey pitch.

PART II

CHAPTER IV
From Farm to Campus

It wasn't always easy for an 18-year-old rural youth from a small high school to adapt to life on a major college campus.

From Heltonville, Bloomington was less than 25 miles through the country, past Bartlettsville, Chapel Hill and Smithville. But the sprawling Indiana University campus could be light years away for someone who had graduated with a class of eight students.

Cladie Bailey made the adjustment, apparently without major difficulty, thanks to a friendly disposition, athletic talent and an ability to adapt to new situations. He would find each of those attributes beneficial over the next 17 years.

Not many young men from the area attended college; some didn't want to, some couldn't afford the cost, it being a time before athletic scholarships and grants. Cladie, however, had informed his parents of his desire to attend college long before his high school graduation.

Jim and Mamie weren't rich, but they managed to set aside what they could—several hundred dollars it is believed—for his expenses.

Parents can sometimes underestimate the spending needs of their children and it was no different with Jim. He complained, in his quiet way, that Cladie spent money too fast.

He informed his son, after the first year, that he could not continue to fully finance his education.

Cladie understood, landed a summer job at the Heltonville Limestone Company in the summer of 1929 and saved his money. The work required him to join the Bloomington Local of the Journeymen Stone Cutters Association, an affiliate of the American Federation of Labor. He kept the union card, long after his work at the company ended, perhaps as a reminder of those difficult years.

He also worked one summer for a timber dealer, hauling logs with Glenard Scott, another Heltonville graduate. "It was day labor, but it gave them something to do and allowed them to make some money which was scarce at the time," Florence Rach Scott, Glendard's widow, recalled.

Bailey augmented his summer earnings as a dishwasher at a sorority house on the I.U. campus. And he watched his funds more closely.

It was there at the sorority house that he would associate for the first time with blacks. The cook was black and Cladie formed a friendship with her that broadened his view of a race he had known little about.

He also joined the campus Reserve Officers Training Corps, a move which gave him extra income and would lead to his commission as a reserve second lieutenant.

By then Cladie was becoming acclimated to the campus, joining the Sigma Pi fraternity which had 36 members pictured in the 1932 "Arbutus." It was just one of a number of Bailey's activities that were mentioned in the campus yearbook.

He had been appointed that year by class president Joseph Zeller to head the tree and ivy planting committee, one of the four major campus committees. Among the seniors he worked with at I.U. was Harold Handley, the class vice president who would eventually become a governor of Indiana.

Bailey played freshman basketball, losing a position on the varsity as a sophomore when some football players with more notable reputations came out after their season ended.

Baseball was now his game. By his junior year, he was on the 21-man roster. As a senior, the "Arbutus" listed Bailey as "one of a powerful hurling trio." By mid-season, one of the other pitchers was in a slump and a second was out with a broken arm. The rest of the season was left to Bailey's strong right arm.

He didn't fail coach Everett Dean, who also was basketball coach. Bailey's effort led to a Big Ten championship and a 13-2 record for the Hoosier baseball team. He was one of 15 players to be awarded varsity letters, receiving a "I" sweater and an all-wool blanket, both of which remain family treasures.

When the team went on the road, Bailey never failed to send a post card to his mother. She preserved them, including one from the team's trip to Mississippi. He was the son every mother would want.

The Bedford newspapers reported his honors. Readers knew then that youths from the playgrounds and cow pastures of small towns of Lawrence County could compete with those from cities with fenced diamonds, dugouts and permanent seats.

Tom Gifford, Indianapolis, lived next door to the Sigma Pi house in Bloomington and knew Bailey well. "We were warm friends during our college days. Most of us never had more than 20 cents in our pockets, but we found a place to play pool and have a good time. I liked him as well as anyone I've known (over the last 70 years)."

Bailey returned to I.U. for a short time to complete his college work, receiving his B.A. degree from I.U. in October, 1933. By then, he would be a teacher and the basketball coach back home in Heltonville.

He took home more than a degree and an honor sweater from Indiana, however. He roomed one year with Caroline Hirst, an elderly lady who soon learned his interest in poetry and literature. She gave him a number of old books, including one about the Yukon which contained Robert Service poetry, which was popular at that time. Bailey memorized those poems, never forgot them and entertained friends for hours by reciting them in the years to come.

* * *

Bailey would continue to play baseball for years. In the summer of 1932 he pitched for Heltonville against teams from communities such as Pinhook, Buddha and Tunnelton.

.   A crowd of 200, sizable for sandlot standards, watched him pitch a 6-4 victory over the Bedford Braves on May 22, 1932. A few days later, Bailey and Bish Wagoner formed the battery when Heltonville broke Pinhook's six-game winning streak on the Pinhook diamond and avenged an earlier loss to the team to the south.

In a double header, Heltonville thumped Buddha 13-2, then had to come back to face Pinhook in the deciding game of their summer series. Pinhook defeated Bailey, who was off form, 11-5. There were reports he had been up late the previous night, perhaps "doing the town," in the parlance of the 1930s, something which wasn't unheard of for young men in their early 20s.

Bailey would continue to play amateur baseball and basketball for the next few years. Sports were a major source of enjoyment in those long days of the Great Depression when money was scarce and entertainment opportunities few.

CHAPTER V

Teacher and Coach

Cladie Bailey wasn't much older than some of his students and athletes when he returned home to Heltonville as a teacher and coach in September 1933.

The students soon learned he expected them to study, concentrate and make the most of their abilities. In return he let them know he was ready to give individual attention to those who needed extra instructions.

It was the same standards he set for his baseball and basketball players. Only those who practiced hard, played with intensity, obeyed his instructions and abided by the rules he set for them remained on his teams.

One of those athletes was Cladie's brother, Jesse. Jesse expected no special treatment and received none. In the gym, and on the diamond, Cladie was his coach, not his brother.

It was a relationship other players appreciated. There would be, they knew, no favorites on either his baseball or basketball teams.

By early October, Bailey had selected the roster for his first basketball team: Jesse, Beryl Turpen, Stanley Patton and Harold Winklepleck, seniors; Boyd Jones, Bert Lewis, Verden Norman, Gene Roberts and Frank Todd, juniors; Ray Chambers, sophomore, and Fred Bailey and Onis Ford freshmen.

The 1933-34 team opened the season October 13 at Clearspring and gave the youthful Bailey an 18-12 victory in his first game as a coach. Brother Jess started at guard.

Two weeks later, the "Blue Jackets," a relatively new team nickname, dumped Freetown, 21-14 at Heltonville. Newspapers reported, "The new Heltonville mentor, Cladie Bailey, played his original starting lineup—Jesse Bailey, Patton, Winklepleck, Roberts and Turpen—the entire game."

Fans had crowded the little gymnasium, filling the seats on the three rows of bleachers that lined each end and one side. Others found standing room in the corners.

It was a time before digital scoreboards, even electric ones at small schools. The score was kept by a student on an enclosed elevated platform, which resembled a pigeon roost, in a corner of the tiny arena. After each basket or free throw, the student inserted the correct score into a slit, changing the numbers with each basket. A circle painted on the front of the scoreboard, between the scores for the home and visiting teams, represented eight minutes, the time in each quarter. The hands on the clock would be moved as the minutes passed to indicate how much time was left in each period. Fans never knew when the time, which was kept at the scorers bench, would expire.

The backboards were wood, unlike the glass ones in big school gyms. Fans would claim for years the caroms off glass was different than off wood, saying that was why the Heltonville team never shot well in the sectionals at Bedford.

Basketball was the king of sports in Indiana and the chief topic of discussions each Saturday morning at the barbershop or wherever men congregated. Bailey had been around town enough to know that he would be second-guessed, but chances are it did not cause him much concern. He had played the game, knew more about it than those who might question his coaching.

On November 1, the Bedford Daily Mail called Heltonville one of the county's stronger teams. But the Seymour Tribune sports writer cautioned Bailey and his team before the Houston game at Clearspring: "Heltonville, you'd better watch those chaps, they are little, but they've got good basket eyes."

Coach Bailey must have listened to the advice. He stressed defense and Heltonville won 28-7.

The victory streak continued. On November 10, Bailey's team defeated Tunnelton 18, 20-18. "Heltonville staved off a last-half rally to overcome their hosts," the newspaper reported. "After trailing 7-5 at the end of the first quarter and a 9-5 at the half, the Indians of Coach Ernest Barnes put on a scoring burst to knot the count at 14 in the third, but lacked two points of standing the pace set by the Blue Jackets in the final stanza."

The schedule was getting more difficult. The Daily Mail in a pre-game story forecast that Heltonville's invasion of Oolitic would bring rivalry to a fever pitch. "The Bearcats haven't won a game yet and Heltonville has lost none. Oolitic expects to get more than one game in the right side of the book before spring and the Mallory gang probably feels that Friday night would be about the ideal time to start the fireworks."

The prediction was correct. Oolitic, the bigger school, won 20-11. The sports writer reported: "Oolitic's fighting Bearcats turned on their traditional steam last night to send an invading Heltonville crew home on the short end of a 20 to 11 score, which represents the first victory of the season for the Mallory boys.

"Heltonville, already having furnished proof that it is a tough basketball outfit, was practically helpless during the first half, which ended with the Bearcats perched on top of a 13 to 4 advantage. In the second half, the Bailey invaders were able to match their hosts point for point but failed to do anything about the nine point advantage Oolitic held at the intermission.

"Along with their difficulty in penetrating the defense zone of the Bearcats, the Bailey lads had a terrible night at the foul line and were able to salvage but one point from 11 charity line pitches. Oolitic hit six of its ten free attempts."

It was just a temporary set back. The next time out, the Heltonville team pounded Williams 44-9. It was an unusually high scoring game and Winklepleck had a season-high 18 points for Bailey's team. The newspaper said: "Heltonville was 35 points better than an invading Williams crew last night and put the banana peels under the visitors." Winklepleck alone doubled the number of points Williams scored, finishing with 18 points, a big scoring night in that era.

There were other tough opponents on the schedule. Heltonville lost its next game to Needmore, 21-17, then was beaten at Fayetteville, 46-24. Few games against county rivals were easy and on occasion games were so rough, referees decided "no blood, no foul." The officials weren't so lenient on this night, the paper reported:

"Thirty-four personal fouls were called during the contest and Heltonville took advantage of the roughness to count 16 points on 24 charity tosses."

The two-game losing streak was soon broken. Bailey's team came back to defeat Tunnelton, 33-9. The Daily Mail had this graphic description:

"Tunnelton's Indians took a heap big licking from an invading Heltonville quintet as Dame Fortune, for the eighth consecutive time, declined to favor the Fortnermen with a smile. No substitution was made in either lineup during the entire game. Only five personals were called, three by Tunnelton, two by Heltonville."

A few days before Christmas, 1933, Heltonville lost to the Bedford Seconds, 28-26. "That friends is something to write home about unless you happen to be from Heltonville," the Daily Mail reported.

The New Year started well. Heltonville defeated Clearspring, 30-21, pulling away in the last few minutes after leading only 18-16 at the end of the third quarter. Its success against Jackson County teams continued when the Blue Jackets defeated

Freetown, 25-16. "Heltonville's triumph adds to the Bailey gang's reputation as a prospective sectional threat," the paper concluded.

When Bailey's team defeated Springville, 37-23, the sports page headline read, "Heltonville wins subless contest." It was becoming apparent that coach Bailey liked his lineup of brother Jesse, Patton, Winklepleck, Roberts and Turpen.

The game story reported, "Coach Bailey's Heltonville hardwoodsmen experienced little difficulty in turning back Springville in a contest which featured the absence of a single change in the starting lineup of either quintet." Patton scored 14 points and Jesse Bailey added 13 points in his best offensive game of the season.

It was a good time to be a Heltonville fan that January of 1934.

* * *

The team's success was overshadowed, however, for a week by news elsewhere. John Dillinger, the Hoosier-born gangster and his men were captured on January 26 at Tucson, Ariz.

The Great Depression was in its depths and Dillinger had become a hero of sorts to some Hoosiers who had lost their savings when banks failed. The Dillinger gang had turned bank robbery into a business, and some people admitted, reluctantly, a vicarious satisfaction at the news of each holdup.

Men who gathered at the barber shop, the restaurant, the general stores or Jerry Jones' feed mill in Heltonville, argued over whether any jail could hold Dillinger.

* * *

It was a topic that continued until the next Friday night. By then, the men's interest had returned to basketball and again they would not be disappointed in Bailey's team.

It breezed to a 59-9 victory over Tunnelton. A week later Heltonville fell to Needmore, 25-22. The Daily Mail called it a hardwood thriller:

"Heltonville's powerful Bailey-coached snipers gave the strong Needmore team plenty of trouble before the latter outfit emerged with a three-point victory. A capacity crowd enjoyed a real bargain in entertainment when Needmore and Heltonville clashed at Heltonville. The invaders led 8-4 at the end of the first quarter and 12-11 at half time and 16-13 as the third installment ended, but the Bailey snipers constantly threatened."

Nothing was certain when county rivals met. Williams edged Heltonville, 17-16, after trailing 12-9 at the half. The victory gave Williams revenge for its earlier loss at Heltonville.

It was time for the season's rematch with Oolitic. Oolitic won, 23-21 in an overtime at Heltonville. The Bedford newspaper reported:

"One of Friday night's closer tilts saw a savage fighting team of Oolitic Bearcats stretch themselves to the limit to turn back Heltonville's powerful machine. Much of the bitterness of the struggle is not suggested by the final count. Heltonville, for example, plunged into offensive methods at the very onset and wound up on the high side of a 12-11 score at the quarter.

Late in the season the Heltonville varsity avenged two earlier season defeats to the Bedford seconds. The first two games were in the Bedford gym. This one was at home. The Blue Jackets held the Bedford reserves scoreless in the first half and took a 15-0 lead, had a 20-2 margin at the end of the third quarter and won 28-11.

It was a good way to end coach Bailey's first regular season.

The luck of the draw matched Heltonville and Oolitic in the first round of the Bedford sectional on February 23, 1934. Oolitic again won, 26-19, in a game that was closer than the score. The newspaper reported:

"Anyone who saw the Bailey crew bow to Oolitic will testify Heltonville put up a mighty game fight. Some observers are of the opinion that Heltonville would have won had some of their better players not been hampered by personal fouls."

Basketball, however, was a secondary story in the Bedford Daily Mail the next day. "DILLINGER ESCAPES JAIL," the headline screamed in 144 point type. The United Press International story explained: "John Dillinger, notorious desperado and bank robber, broke out of the Lake County (Indiana) jail today and escaped in the private automobile of sheriff Lillian Holley."

Dillinger's daring act, perpetrated with a make-believe gun fashioned from soap and blackened with shoe polish, make the sectional a secondary story.

* * *

Ray Chambers was a sophomore reserve on Bailey's 1934 team. "He (Cladie) threw me a varsity uniform before the first game and I felt about nine feet tall. I played on the reserve team most of the time, but I did get into some varsity games.

"I played under four different coaches, Lawrence Thompson as a freshman, Cladie as a sophomore, Ray Julian, as a junior, and Ray Fry as a senior. Cladie was the best I played for in those four years. There's no doubt about it.

"I never heard him talk about anybody in a bad way. If he didn't have something good to say about a person, he wouldn't say anything. If a player wasn't very good, Cladie would try to make the game as much fun for the kid as he could."

Chambers called Bailey strict and added: "He was a disciplinarian, but he didn't harp on it all the time. You went by his rules and he'd get on you if you didn't follow them. If you went out and worked, you had a chance to play. The fact his brother, Jesse, was on the team rankled some of the players at first, but not for long once they learned that the coach would treat everyone the same. If you did your job," Chambers recalled, "you got to play, regardless of who you were."

Jesse knew from the start he would receive no favors from his brother. "It was kind of a strain in some ways, but he (Cladie) was fair with every one. I didn't want any favors and he didn't give me any. I had to earn a place on the team just like anyone else.

"I've never forgotten what he told me: 'You can do what you want to away from school, but when you go on that floor you will do what I want you to or you'll be sitting beside me on the bench.' So it was up to me whether I would play or not.

"And he stayed with that! At that time he didn't make any rules, but he made it clear: 'You can play as long as you play to suit me. If you don't produce on the floor you won't play.'

"As I recall we won about 12 games that year and lost about six. I think all the boys liked him pretty well and that includes about every one who ever played for him in any sport or any year," Jesse explains.

Cladie Bailey lived at home that season and he and Jesse usually walked home together after games and practices. Jesse would complain, jokingly, a half century later that he couldn't enjoy a smoke on those walks because the coach was with him. (Father Jim had a car at that time, but he didn't drive it much except to his carpentry jobs.)

Both Jesse and Ray Chambers played baseball for Cladie's high school team, where his standards were the same.

* * *

Cladie Bailey showed no favoritism in the classroom, either, recalls Nora Trogdon Todd, who was a seventh grader in Bailey's health class that year. He was a distant relative she had known as a neighbor since birth. She admits she didn't do much home work the first grading period, expecting, she recalled 50 years later, that Bailey would show her some favoritism.

She was wrong. He wrote "D" on her report card. She knew then she would need to study harder to earn a better grade. She did and her grades improved. It was obvious that Bailey expected his students, as well as his players, to work.

He would, however, spend time with individual students if they needed extra help. Mary Helen Bridwell Sproles recalls she often had trouble with mathematics. Rather than see her fail, Bailey would work with her in class until he knew she could pass each test.

CHAPTER VI

The Depression Years

The rookie coach had done well, returning to his home town to coach a team that won twice as many games as it lost. So it was assumed Bailey would return after the successful season. That would not be the case.

Bailey preferred adventure to the sometimes dull formality of speeches and lectures. That likely is why he skipped the State Teachers Institute at Indianapolis in the fall of 1933, even though attendance was considered mandatory at the time. Instead he and Fred Maher, another teacher at Heltonville, chose to attend the 1933 World's Fair at Chicago, which likely was more educational.

There are conflicting stories about why Bailey was not rehired, but his absence from those institute sessions likely was part of the reason.

Fred Maher, the nephew of principal W. C. Roberts, however, kept his job, even though Bailey didn't, an indication that nepotism existed even then.

Cladie's brother, Jesse, has a slightly different version. "I hadn't heard about the World's Fair, or, if I had, I had forgotten it," he said. "As I recall, Fred and Clade taught the same subjects so one of them had to be let go. I think that had more to do with it. Anyhow, Fred went ahead and taught and Clade was let out. We always thought W. C. Roberts, who had been hired by Jack Clark (the township trustee), was the one who made the decision not to rehire Clade."

* * *

The Bailey story was just one of the topics of conversations around Heltonville that scorching summer of 1934. Times were hard, so was the ground, for rains came only sporadically. Crops withered, pastures turned brown and wells ran dry. There was no air conditioning and little relief from what was called the most intense heat wave in the history of the state. "Hell on earth," some folks called it.

Only a sensational development could over take the weather as the most discussed issue of that July. That incident came on July 22 when John Dillinger was shot and killed as he left a theater in Chicago. "It was the end," the Associated Press wrote, "of the incredible crime career of the internationally-known hoodlum."

* * *

Crime, depression and the weather may have dominated the news that summer, but there were omens, perhaps even more distressing, in other parts of the world.

Rep. E.B. Crowe, a Democrat from Bedford, returned from a visit to Hawaii, and warned a gathering in his home town that the island territory was almost defenseless.

Pearl Harbor's defense, he said, relied on howitzers which were old even before World War I. The Japanese, he observed, would have no trouble taking the islands. Crowe would continue to be critical of Hawaii's defense in the years ahead. No one paid enough attention to do anything about it.

Men like Cladie Bailey would later pay a price for that inattention.

* * *

Cladie Bailey had taught and coached on a permit that first year at Heltonville. He would return to college later to complete his accreditation for a teaching degree.

Bailey's decision to join the Reserve Officers Training Corps while a student at Indiana University had led to his commission as a second lieutenant in the Army Reserve. The commission would be helpful to him in the peaceful, but depressed 1930s.

The Great Depression of that decade left millions of young men broke and jobless and led to the creation of the Civilian Conservation Corps in 1933. Congress authorized funds to establish camps and hire unemployed men between 17 and 25 whose families were on relief. Those chosen were assigned to work on conservation projects across America in a massive effort to restore and preserve farm and timberland.

The men were paid $30 a month, $25 of which was sent home to their families. They could spend the $5 at the camp canteen to buy candy, cigarettes and toiletries. Work schedules were basically the same at all work camps: Wake up call at 5:30 a.m. A hot breakfast at 6 a.m. Go to work at 7:15 a.m.

Free medical and dental care was provided. So was clothing, both for leisure wear and for work.

Leisure time was to be used in study and recreation, "best suited," the guidelines read, "to the boy's needs and desires of each boy." Classroom instruction was offered.

Congress had directed that discipline was to be maintained "by example and persuasion." Penalties for infractions of rules were to be mostly confined to fines, extra duties or, in extreme cases, dishonorable discharge.

Camps, usually barracks, were under command of the Army even though no military training was permitted. The men, however, were required to be prompt, obedient, orderly and to take orders.

Field work was under supervision of civilians assigned to ECW (Emergency Conservation Work). Men with ROTC commissions could apply for active Army duty and be assigned to CCC units. Cladie Bailey was one of those who did, probably because a lieutenant was paid $2,400 a year, almost three times what a teacher, if employed, could make at that time.

One of Bailey's assignments was in northeastern Indiana at a camp near Bluffton. He would serve a total of about two years with the CCC from 1935 to 1937, his brothers Bill and Jesse recalled.

(Exact dates of Bailey's service as an Army officer assigned to CCC units are not available. Those records were destroyed in a fire along with 16 million other files in a fire at the National Personnel Records Center in St. Louis on July 12, 1973).

In rural areas of northern Indiana, the CCC units were assigned to clean open drainage ditches through the fertile prairie-like fields. It was a new experience for youths who came from the major cities of the Midwest.

"He had a lot of young men out of Chicago who didn't seem to care what they did. They were kind of hard to control sometimes and Clade didn't have the authority he would have over men in military service. They'd sign up for duty, then take off and would have to be hunted down," Jesse recalls.

Despite the problems some of the men caused, the CCC was considered a success. In addition to drainage ditch work, tile lines were laid, erosion control projects were completed, trees planted and fences repaired.

As the depression eased, the CCC camps were phased out. Young men who had battled erosion and fought to improve the nation's soil would soon be engaged in a war to protect the country's freedom.

For Cladie Bailey, who would be promoted to a first lieutenant during his tours with the CCC, it would widen his experience as a leader of men and give him an edge over other officers when the Army activated him a few years later for a more dangerous assignment.

* * *

Seasons changed, years passed, and the Great Depression remained. Jobs were difficult to find and young men, who might have left had times been better, continued to live at home.

Bailey, who remained close to his parents, had no full time job the summer of 1938, but he wasn't idle. He would talk later about the hours he spent helping his mother, Mamie, preserve what they had grown in the garden. "We canned every thing we could get our hands on," he would recall.

Some men that age might have bristled at the thought of helping with a household chore. Bailey knew, however, that a man's character could be judged by the way he treated his mother and he did not complain.

Canning, at the time, was not easy. The Bailey home still had no electricity, no running water, and the work had to be done over an outdoor fire or inside over a wood-heated kitchen range. What was canned was stored in the cellar, a dugout between the house and the barn,, to be consumed over the long winter ahead.

When Bailey returned at night from sports events or visits to town he entered the house through a back door into the kitchen, usually in search of a cold biscuit or a snack.

If he walked in when food was cooking, he often lifted the lid to see what he would have for supper. His mom later revealed that on more than one occasion he scalded his nose with a lid even though he was an adult at the time.

* * *

Bailey continued to spend his leisure time on the baseball diamonds in the summer, the basketball hardwoods in the winter. When he was not on active duty with the Civilian Conservation Corps, he found work at whatever jobs were available.

"Clade, during that time (of the depression)," brother Jesse recalls, "was about like all the rest of us. He ran around here, there and yonder, working a little, going to school some. It was a rough time for people.

"Clade didn't think he was above anybody, or that anyone was above him. He treated people like he would like to be treated."

PART III

CHAPTER VII
Return to Coaching

After a five-year absence, Cladie Bailey returned as a teacher and coach at Heltonville in September, 1939, succeeding his friend, Marshall George, who moved to Needmore.

George had been a popular coach, leading the Blue Jackets to an 11-8 record the previous year, but fans were excited about Bailey's return. He hadn't left the area and he remained a home town favorite.

Classes started on Tuesday after Labor Day, three days after the German army had rolled into Poland. Soon most of Europe would be involved in the World War II madness created by Adolf Hitler.

Although five varsity players had graduated, Bailey looked forward to rebuilding a contender around veterans Earl Lantz, Norval Tanksley and Mack Todd.

Pat Bailey, an underclassman and the coach's cousin, became a starter and one of the team's leading scorers. The roster also included Earl Lantz's brother, Doyle, Leroy Morris and freshman Bob Hillenberg.

Bailey's team opened the season on November 3 by pounding Huron, 40-8, and eased by Tunnelton, 20-18. The team continued to play well until Christmas, winning over Springville and Freetown, losing to Needmore, Shawswick and Fayetteville.

Bailey knew Earl Lantz's eligibility would end in mid-season when he reached his 20th birthday. He also knew it would be unfair to deny Lantz an opportunity to play as long as he could, even though it would mean he would have to be replaced at a crucial point in the schedule.

Lantz was the team's most consistent player, a skilled ball handler at his guard position. Bailey moved sophomore Loren Henderson into the starting line up and he offset some of the scoring loss.

The team, however, never regained its early-season momentum, lost to Shawswick, 35-26, in the county tourney, and dropped three of its last four regular season games. It then was upset in the sectional at Mitchell, losing to Williams, 33-28, in the opening round.

No one, certainly not the players, blamed Bailey for the late-season losses. All agreed he should return for another season. This time both the coach and the players would see their wish granted.

Earl Lantz remembers Bailey as a disciplinarian. "You did what he said or you didn't play. Once he said something, he wanted you to do it right the first time and continue to do it that way. And he could show you how he wanted things done, having been a great player himself. I often stayed after practice to shoot free throws with him. He was a great shooter."

After Lantz became too old to play on the varsity, he joined coach Bailey on an independent team coached by Walter "Dutch" Holt. With Bailey and Lantz in the same line up, the team seldom lost.

Lantz had played independent baseball in the summer of 1939 on a team coached by Bailey. "I remember one game when I misplayed a couple of flies out in the field. I came in and said, 'I quit!' Cladie looked at me, smiled and asked, 'How can you quit? You haven't started yet.' That's the way he was. He could get his point across in a way that didn't hurt your feelings. Cladie was one great guy. As an Army officer, I bet he was the greatest," Earl Lantz adds. Like Lantz, soldiers would learn that Bailey was a leader on the battlefield as he had been on the hardwood.

* * *

Mack Todd, who played on Cladie's 1939-40 team, still refers to him as "Mr. Bailey" and calls him a good coach.

He recalls Bailey worked "long and hard" with individual players, teaching them how best to shoot free throws, use head fakes, drive, dribble and pass. "He would never leave the gym at night as long as there was a single player who wanted to improve his game.

"He wanted to win, but he would not allow you to play if you were sick. I recall that one of the players got sick while playing because he had eaten just before a game. After that, Mr. Bailey told the players to wait until after the games were over to eat and offered to buy each of us a sandwich on the way home when we returned from other schools. The promise of food gave us motivation to win at places like Huron and Springville. When we won, we would stop at a Sandwich Shop on "J" Street in Bedford. Teachers and coaches didn't make much at the time, but he always treated us, even if he had to borrow money to do it.

"Mr. Bailey didn't rant and rave, but he took the game of basketball seriously. He wanted the game played his way and there was very little humor in the gym when it wasn't done that way."

* * *

Bailey also coached the school's baseball and softball teams. As in basketball, he required his players to be in good physical condition. Anyone who wasn't, didn't play.

Bailey's experience as a player and coach allowed him to recognize an individual's weakness and to give one-on-one instructions.

"With me," Mack Todd recalls, "it was the curve ball. He would always say 'watch the ball. Look at the ball.' And sometimes he could be real emphatic on what he wanted."

Bailey's 1940 softball team lost, 11-7, to Fayetteville in the county softball tournament, but losses on the diamond were not as important as losses on the hardwood to the rabid basketball fans of that era.

CHAPTER VIII

The Men of Summer

Bailey continued to play, and usually coach, baseball and softball teams in different leagues over the summers, Todd recalls. He was taking graduate classes at I.U. at night, and cutting weeds on a road crew by days, but he still found time to coach and play.

One of the teams Bailey coached was the Heltonville "400" team in the Lawrence-Jackson Baseball League, a conference that also included the Heltonville Merchants, Huron, Tunnelton, Kurtz, Bedford Cubs, Shawswick and the Bedford Boys Club.

The "400" team played on a diamond in the Leatherwood Creek bottoms off Ind. 58 between Heltonville and Bedford. The Heltonville Merchants' home diamond was a field on the Homer Duncan farm near Zelma.

Cladie, whose arm was showing the effect of hundreds of innings, would not pitch often during the season, but his play at second base and his clutch hitting would remain an asset.

The "400" team, with Dale Sowder on the mound, opened the season with a 10-6 loss to Tunnelton. That loss, however, would not be an indication of the season to come. The team came back to score a 6-3 non-league victory over Mitchell and continued to win. Bailey came on in relief when the team defeated the Bedford Cubs, 12-4. Victories were frequent, defeats seldom, that season.

Bailey's team won the State Amateur Baseball sectional at Tunnelton in August, 1940, a fete reported in the Bedford Daily Mail:

"Twelve members of the Heltonville 400 baseball team depart Saturday at 5 a.m. for Kokomo, where they will compete in the State Amateur tournament over the weekend. The team will face Lizton in the first round.

"On the roster are Manager Cladie Bailey, second baseman (.361 hitting average); Rollie Walls, first baseman (.565); Paul Potts, outfielder and pitcher (.359); John Bailey, outfielder (.387); G. L. Scott, outfielder (.407); Loren Henderson, infielder (.267); Mack Todd, outfielder (.317), Dale Sowder, pitcher (.230); Ollie Mann, infielder, (.250); Ray Chambers, outfielder (.235), and Walter "Dutch" Holt, utility player (.287)."

Also in the tournament were an Indianapolis team, plus Knox, Lizton, South Bend, East Chicago, Kokomo, Austin and Shelbyville.

The Daily Mail reported following the Labor Day weekend: "After winning their first game, the Heltonville 400 sectional amateur baseball champions, bowed out of the state finals at Kokomo after the second game.

"Heltonville defeated Lizton, 11-9, in the initial tilt Saturday morning, then lost to Shelbyville, 5-4, in a game that started at 8:30 a.m. Sunday.

"Sowder opened the Lizton game but was relieved in the second inning by Bailey, who finished and was credited with the win. Paul Potts was the hurler for the second game, working with fine results, but his mates were unable to push across the tying or winning runs."

Potts never forgot those summers of 1939 and 1940 when he played for Bailey. "He was pretty much a gentleman. He was low key and I don't recall ever hearing him swear or lose his temper.

"There was another Bailey (John, a cousin) who played on that team. John liked to honky tonk a little bit on Saturday nights and he came out with a hangover one Sunday. Cladie wouldn't let him play, which caused a few words to be exchanged. Cladie didn't get loud or anything like that. He just let John know that he was the manager and that John was in no condition to play. And John didn't play, which showed Cladie's control over the team.

"Everybody liked Cladie. He was older than a lot of us were, so we respected and looked up to him. I remember we were playing Tunnelton one day when a couple of the players started to fight. Cladie put a stop to that pretty quick."

By the time another season rolled around, Bailey was in the Army and Dale Sowder was "drafted" to play for the Bedford A's, a semi pro team.

CHAPTER IX

Apple of His Eyes

It had been a busy month for Cladie Bailey. The baseball team's season had been important, but it likely, in his mind, was overshadowed by two other events.

He had signed a contract on August 8 to return to Heltonville for another school year. The contract, issued by trustee William J. "Jack" Clark, would pay him $1,040 to teach and coach for the eight-month term.

Nine days later on August 17, he would meet Katherine Hobson, an attractive 18-year-old redhead from Bedford.

Katherine would not forget that date. She explained how they met: "We lived on North "I" Street in Bedford and I had gone downtown with a cousin. At that time, nearly all the young people congregated around the Courthouse Square on Saturday nights.

"We hadn't been there long when we saw Sam Bailey and his wife, Mildred, whom I knew. Sam asked me if I would have a date with his cousin. I first said, 'No, I don't believe so. Besides Cynthia is here with me.'

"Sam had an answer for that. He said Loren Fish wants a date too and he can go out with Cynthia." He then told Katherine, "My cousin is standing down in front of the pool room on the West side of the square if you want to see what he looks like."

It was then Katherine suggested that Sam and Mildred go first and that she and Cynthia would walk behind. She told Sam, "You speak to your cousin so I'll know who he is."

Katherine was pleased with what she saw. "He (Cladie) was so neat looking in a starched white shirt with his sleeves turned up, that being how young men dressed at the time."

Sam would later joke that Katherine stepped on his heels when she saw Cladie and yelled, "I'll go, I'll go." It would be the first of dozens of dates over the next eight months.

One of the first places Cladie took Katherine was to a "400" baseball game. "I was eating a little old green apple when the game ended," she recalls. "He asked if I liked those things (green apples). I said I did. The next time he picked me up he had a big green apple in the car for me."

The days of Bailey the bachelor were numbered.

CHAPTER X

Character Builder

Bailey returned to the classroom that September and it was there he had as great an impact on the lives of students as he did on his basketball players.

One of Bailey's math students was Frank Hunter, who lived on a farm southeast of Heltonville. Hunter had too many chores to do each morning and night to play sports, but he recalled the role Bailey, the teacher, played in his life.

Hunter later became a teacher, principal and eventually superintendent of the Perry Township school system in suburban Marion County, Indiana.

He called Bailey, "A super guy." "Not everyone who teaches is that well thought of by students. He was an excellent teacher, the kind we are told today (1994) that we should have. He really was interested in the kids and that was reflected when he spent a greater amount of his time with individuals rather than in front of the class lecturing. Unlike some teachers, he didn't tell students to open their books and see what they could get out of them.

"Looking back, I recall that he spent time helping a student as a person. He knew enough about Heltonville to know that kids who grew up in the country in that era might have trouble finding a place in life as adults. He sort of looked for people, I thought, who might be better off if they gave up farm life. He would sit down and talk to us about those types of things. He would tell us what he had done, how he had done it, explaining that we could succeed if we chose to take paths that would lead us away from Heltonville."

Hunter, who would observe hundreds of educators in his own career, called Bailey "a different kind of person than most teachers." It was a compliment Bailey would have appreciated.

Nellie Trogdon Mikels, who graduated with Hunter in 1943, admits she was not a good math student until she was taught by Bailey. He had a way of making algebra easier than she thought, explained it so she could grasp what he taught.

"I remember getting A's and B's, but I'm not sure I was that smart," she insists.

* * *

September's 30 days seemed much longer for basketball players waiting for the start of practice October 1. Chances are the days passed as slowly for Bailey.

Bob Wray, who graduated in 1941, didn't play basketball, but he recalls watching Bailey when the students played in the gymnasium at noon.

"He would stand at the center of the floor, launch his two-handed shots which would rip through the basket, flipping the net up through the rim. It amazed me at that age. I was awe struck by it and I remembered those shots and reran them in my mind years later." It would be a poignant recollection.

Those shooting exhibitions helped Bailey pass the time until basketball season started.

Mack Todd and Norval Tanksley had graduated from the 1939-40 team and again Bailey would have to rebuild his team.

Pat Bailey and Loren Henderson, starters from the previous year, were back as were Doyle Lantz, Dale Stultz, Bob Hillenberg and sophomores Opal Todd, Roscoe Adamson, Dale Norman and Gerald Denniston.

In a pre-season story, the Bedford Daily Mail reported that Bailey, in his practices, had "concentrated on speed and drive in the hope of overcoming a somewhat distressing lack of size."

The Blue Jackets opened the season on the road, defeating Huron, 23-21. "Play was fast and furious at times on the small Huron floor," the newspaper reported.

A week later, Bailey's team was at home, losing to Tunnelton, 30-25, in what was called "a nip and tuck struggle." Henderson had 13 points to lead all scorers.

By then, the manual scoreboard in the corner of the gym was gone, replaced by an electronic board placed high over a new stage on one side of the gym. Technology had come to Heltonville.

Heltonville then fell at Williams, 21-14, in what the Daily Mail called "the upset in the county."

The team evened its record at 2-2 when it defeated Needmore, 29-26. Loren Henderson, who with Bailey would do most of the scoring during the season, had 17 points.

Neighboring Shawswick was Heltonville's biggest rival in that era and every game was a struggle. It would be no different when Bailey's team played the Farmers early in the season. Shawswick, coached by Ward Smith, whose teams at various schools would win hundreds of games over four decades, defeated Heltonville, 24-14, before what the newspaper called "a howling home crowd."

Bob Hillenberg recalls an incident from that game. "Opal Todd and Johnny Mathis of Shawswick seemed to get into a fight every time we played. It was no different that night." What was different was Bailey's reaction. "He put a stop to that on the spot. 'I'll take care of any fighting. You just play,' he told Ope."

County teams usually met twice each season and Heltonville would avenge the loss in a few weeks.

Meantime it lost for the second time to Williams, 29-23, then came back to crush Huron, 36-16, in a game in which

Henderson scored 13 points. He added 10 when the team gained revenge against Tunnelton, winning 25-20.

* * *

No one was happier when Heltonville won than Katherine Hobson, who by then was attending most of the team's games.

For single female teachers at Heltonville, who might have had their eyes on Bailey, it was time for them to look elsewhere.

A case in point came when one female teacher, pretty and shapely with dark hair and an object of stares from her male students, wanted to date Bailey. She asked a male teacher and his wife to arrange a bridge game to which she and the coach would be invited. Bailey went to the card game, but left as soon as the hands had been played, then relayed the incident to Katherine, who would confess:

"He seemed to want to date me. Which was all right with me."

Bailey was an imposing figure that season, almost six feet tall in street shoes, neatly groomed, well dressed, often in a dark suit between a blue and a green in color with vague stripes. In the final pre-game huddle, he would reach into a side pocket of his coat, pull out a package of chewing gum and hand a stick to each of the starters. Gum could help relieve the jitters.

The coach also was concerned about his players off the court, too. Katherine remembers that Bailey was concerned about Opal Todd's language. "I just can't get him to stop swearing," he told her more than once.

She would not forget Todd or Loren Henderson, who was called "Boob." "I can remember him talking about those two players. The others teased Cladie so much about me, maybe, I didn't want to hear too much about them."

* * *

Heltonville entered the county tourney with a 4-9 record. It fell, 34-24, to a powerful Springville team that would eventually win the title. Bailey was beginning to see some improvement in his team, despite the loss.

That improvement was more evident a week later when the team crushed Van Buren, a team from Brown County, 61-16. Henderson scored 20 points, a season high.

Heltonville fans were even happier a week later when the Blue Jackets defeated Shawswick, 16-15, holding the Farmers scoreless in the final quarter. This time the game was at home and any howling was done by the Heltonville fans who filled every seat and stood in corners and entry ways.

The team closed the season, losing again to Springville despite Henderson's 14 points. By then Bailey was calling Henderson the best dribbler he had seen, and few rival coaches disagreed.

It was obvious Heltonville, with standouts like Henderson and Pat Bailey, was better than its record. It was well coached, had lost a number of close games, and seldom had been outclassed.

CHAPTER XI

A Game to Remember

The sectional pairings matched Heltonville and Needmore in the first round. The two teams had split their regular season games, but Needmore, which had played well in the county tourney, was expected by most observers to win.

No one in the big assembly room over the gymnasium doubted coach Bailey that morning when he told the 100 or so junior-senior high students at Heltonville:

"We will beat Needmore in the sectional tonight." It wasn't a boast. It was a simple, clear and precise comment, as exact as answers to the math problem he gave his classes.

"Tonight" was Friday, February. 28, 1941, a time when the nation was at peace, but the world wasn't, an era when basketball was king in small town Indiana.

Bailey's comment was more of a declaration than a boast, an affirmation of sorts despite his team's 7-12 record. Others might have been skeptical, but not his players, not the students, not the Blue Jacket fans.

Sports writers for the two Bedford daily newspapers had made Needmore the favorite, but they didn't know Bailey's ability to inspire his players to over achieve.

Bailey didn't make promises he didn't expect to keep. Bob Hillenberg knew it, so did Pat Bailey, Loren Henderson, Opal Todd and Dale Norman, the other starters at season's end.

Bailey had the team ready to play. Hillenberg knew the players were up for the game. "It's win or else. Or else, we let the coach down," he thought as the students cheered Bailey's pronouncement.

The players liked their coach, appreciated what he had taught them in the gymnasium as well as in the classroom, had seen him more as an older brother than an authoritarian figure.

Bailey's promise had motivated them, given them the self-assurance they may have lacked. By game time they were ready. Like Hillenberg, the others vowed to keep Bailey's word. It would, they agreed, be their best effort of the season They would not lose, they convinced themselves.

It appeared for much of the game that Heltonville's best would not be good enough. Needmore led 6-4 after one quarter, 11-6 at the half and was still in front, 17-15, late in the game. No matter! Bailey's team had a promise to keep.

Henderson, a junior, sank a fielder, to knot the score. Pat Bailey and Norman added a free throw each to give Heltonville a 19-17 victory.

An upset, some called it. Not his players, especially Bob Hillenberg. "We knew when the coach said something he meant for us to do it," he would say later.

Heltonville would meet Bedford in the semifinal the next afternoon and lose as expected. Bailey was a realist. He had made no promise of a second victory. A triumph against the big county seat school, he knew, was likely beyond his team's capability.

The defeat to Bedford, however, would not dim the upset of Needmore. That would be a game—and a promise—that the players and the fans would never forget.

Neither Bailey nor his players knew it at the time, but it would be the last time he would have the opportunity to coach.

* * *

Bailey, being an outstanding player himself, expected a lot out of his players, Hillenberg had learned after two seasons. "He wanted the best we had to give. He was strict with his rules and if you didn't follow them you didn't play. Roscoe Adamson learned that.

"Cladie wanted us in by 9 p.m. the night before a game and if he heard you weren't, you were off the team. That's what happened to Roscoe. I always abided by the rules because I wanted to play.

"Cladie had been a good outside shooter and he always tried to show us what was considered the proper shooting method back then. 'Snap your wrist. Snap your wrist,' I heard him say I don't know how many times.

"He was just a good all around coach. He was hard in practice and he put us through a lot of difficult work. He knew his basketball, he knew how to teach it and how to get the best out of each player. When we didn't win, he was kind of down on us, but he didn't hold a grudge."

Having grown up in the area, Bailey knew the backgrounds of his players, knew what problems they had. "He seemed like one of us," Hillenberg remembers.

Hillenberg has never forgotten an incident that was an example of Bailey the man. "After away games, we'd always eat at a restaurant on the West side of the square in Bedford. Each time the waitresses gave each of us a ticket we were to turn over to Clade, so he could pay all the bills at one time. One night some of the players slipped out with their tickets instead of giving them to Cladie, bragging to each other that they had eaten free. When the coach learned what had happened he gave the entire team a lecture about honesty. I mean he really chewed us out. It never happened again. That has always stayed in my mind."

The team may have upset Bailey on and off the court, but he never used foul or obscene language, Hillenberg says. And he didn't allow his players to use profanity or to fight.

Hillenberg confirmed what Frank Hunter had said about Bailey, that he was as great a teacher in the classroom as he was in the gymnasium. "He was able to relate information in a way you could comprehend, whether it was in a math or bookkeeping class. It was the same on the basketball floor. He could stand there and show how the plays should be run, then go through them himself."

Hillenberg called Bailey "a good teacher. He took time to explain a subject so it was understandable. He spent a lot of time with individual students. Opal Todd, for example, had some trouble with math, I recall, and he (Cladie) spent a lot of time with Opal."

* * *

Bailey had not only coached the high school varsity that season, he also had the reserve and junior high teams.

Wayne Trogdon, who had helped Cladie dig that silo pit back in August, was a seventh-grader on the junior high team. The team didn't practice too often because of Bailey's overloaded schedule, but it was an experience Wayne would appreciate more as the years passed.

"We won about half our games," he recalls, explaining that "we" were himself, John Earl Todd, Dale Hawkins, Richard Bartlett and Russell Lantz.

"At basketball practice and in the classroom Bailey was always serious. He had his jaws locked and tolerated no foolishness. There probably were 10 other boys in my class in 40-41. One time one of us got out of line and Cladie wasn't sure who was the guilty one. So he took all of us to the office and each of us got three pretty good licks with a paddle to make sure he had punished the guilty student."

(Cladie and Katherine Hobson were sitting in Bailey's 1939 Chevy on the square in Bedford one night when a boy about 12 or 13 walked by, waved and laughed. He returned in a few minutes and banged on the window. He wanted to be sure Clade saw him. When he left, Bailey laughed and told his date, "That's one of the boys I spanked." That boy was John Earl Todd, who later married into the Bailey family, becoming the husband of one of Cladie's nieces.

("I don't know what the boys had done, but Clade spanked them instead of asking Mr. Raines, the principal, to do it," Katherine related later.)

Trogdon adds, "At a junior high game at Shawswick, some of the Shawswick varsity players were razzing John Earl and me pretty good. We started giving them some lip in return. After the game, Cladie said, 'Never again! I will do the talking and fighting. You do the playing.'"

It was the same lesson Opal Todd also had learned in the varsity game at Shawswick earlier in the season and was additional evidence that Bailey was consistent, treated everyone alike, had no favorites.

Wayne Trogdon can, a half century later, vividly recall the man who was his first coach. "Cladie almost always wore a hat with the brim turned up all the way around. He carried himself erect, proudly and was always neat in appearance."

He can also remember his coach's kindness. "He had a 1939 Chevy, a two-door sedan, and he often took Dale Hawkins and me home. He was living with his parents on Ind. 58 at the time and our homes were out of his way. We always hoped he didn't have a date those nights because if he had we both would have to walk the five miles."

The "dates" Bailey might have had were, of course, with Katherine Hobson. The romance was growing more serious as the season passed.

* * *

All 12 grades attended the Heltonville school at that time. Before students were to have their picture taken one day that winter, coach Bailey observed Wilma Bailey, a niece who was in elementary school, had chocolate smeared over her mouth. He washed her face, fixed her hair and saw to it she would appear well groomed for the camera. Wilma, who was the daughter of James Bailey, probably still wonders what she would have looked like in that picture if her uncle hadn't been there.

CHAPTER XII

A Call to Serve

It had been a winter when America began to mobilize for war. In January, work was underway at the new Burns City Naval Depot west of Bedford and hundreds of men sought employment there. Other men who had endured the idleness of the Great Depression took jobs at the giant ammunition depot at Charlestown to the southeast.

Basketball season ended, spring arrived and war clouds darkened the blue skies of southern Indiana. Young men, like Harold Lantz who reported for duty April 9, were being drafted. Reserve Army officers were summoned to active duty. Bailey knew it was only a matter of time before he would be back in uniform.

His call to serve his country came in early April. He was ordered to report on Saturday, April 19, two weeks before school was out for the year.

Frank Hunter recalls the reaction of students: "I remember how disappointed we were when we learned that he was being activated. It was a loss to us sophomores, knowing he wouldn't be there for our last two years of high school."

April 19 was a day when newspapers reported that Adolph Hitler's Balkan blitz had pushed into Greece past Mount Olympus. The U.S. remained at peace.

Bailey left without much fanfare. An item under "Flatwoods News" in the Bedford Daily Times reported: "Claude (neighborhood news at that time usually was hand scripted by a correspondent who mailed newspapers copy that was difficult for linotype operators to read) Bailey will leave for the Army Saturday. A family dinner in his honor was given Sunday at his parents' home."

A few days later, Richard Rainbolt, a sports writer for the Daily Times, revealed that Robert Barrett, former Springville coach, would be the new basketball coach at Heltonville.

"This word comes immediately following the departure of Cladie Bailey, native Heltonvillian, who led the Blue Jackets the past two seasons and has now entered the United States Army."

Bailey's pre-induction physical showed he was 70 3/4ths inches tall, 165 pounds, 32 inches at the waist. "Scar on left arm —July 3, 1934—when car key broke off. Healed in a week," the overworked examining physician wrote, cryptically.

Lieutenant Cladie Bailey was soon on his way to Camp Livingston, La., to join the 32nd Infantry Division, a National Guard unit made up mostly of men from Wisconsin and northern Michigan.

* * *

At Camp Livingston, Bailey would be reunited with O. O. Dixon, whom he had known since high school. The two, by coincidence, had almost identical backgrounds.

They grew up no more than five miles apart in Lawrence County. Cladie had been an athlete at Heltonville, Dixon at Tunnelton. Both graduated from Indiana University, Dixon a year earlier than Bailey. Both had taught school, mostly mathematics, both had been on active duty with the Civilian Conservation Corps. Dixon was ordered to active duty on May 1, 1941, also as a lieutenant 11 days after Bailey, and also was sent to Camp Livingston.

Dixon would recall later that the 126th Infantry Regiment of the 32nd Division, being a National Guard unit, was "not disposed kindly" to any ROTC officers. "It was a clannish atmosphere. I remember I reported to the base with a friend after dark and it was raining. We were told to go to the tent at the end of the third row. That was the treatment we got."

It was likely Bailey received similar treatment. That would change for both he and Dixon in the months to come as both won the respect and admiration of those who had looked upon ROTC graduates with suspicion.

* * *

Cladie Bailey and Katherine Hobson had dated for eight months when they decided it was time for her to meet his parents. By then they both knew they would likely marry, although no date had been set.

Mamie Bailey welcomed Katherine and would say later, "It must be serious because he brought her home to meet us." She also noted that Katherine looked a lot like Helen, Cladie's sister who was the youngest in the family.

Teaching and coaching had kept Cladie busy during the school year, but he found time to take Katherine to movies in Bedford and on dates to Bloomington. "Sometimes Sam and Mildred would pick me up and take me to the basketball games," she recalls.

Their romance continued by mail once he left for Camp Livingston. In June, Lieutenant Bailey wrote to his parents that he and Katherine would be married. Mamie and Jim were pleased.

PART IV

CHAPTER XIII
Tragedy at Home

Baseball would not be the same around Heltonville that spring or summer. Cladie Bailey was in the Army, so were some other members of the "400" team, which disbanded. A few of the players, such as pitcher Dale Sowder, joined other teams.

The Heltonville Merchants started the season back at the diamond east of town. That, too, would end suddenly, tragically, on May 18.

It was a warm sunny Sunday and Junior, Frank, Jim, Chuck and Froggy planned to make the most of it. They would, they decided, walk four miles east on Ind. 58 from their homes near Heltonville, relax in the sun and watch the Merchants play.

They had plenty of time so they moseyed along, exchanging banter, kidding each other as only friends could. They shuffled their feet along the blacktop, its oil oozing in the sun.

They were just a half-mile from the ball park as they approached a hill on the road. Chances are their hands were in their pockets, clinging tightly to the coins they planned to use to buy soft drinks that would be sold from a tub cooled with chunks of ice.

Suddenly an eastbound car approached from behind. Another came down the hill from the opposite direction. Both drivers attempted to avoid the pedestrians. The cars sideswiped, sending one caroming into Junior, Frank, Jim, Chuck and Froggy.

When the wreckage was cleared, Junior, Frank and Jim were dead. Chuck and Froggy were injured. So were seven other people in the two cars, including Marshall Axsom, one of the drivers who had taught at Heltonville, was a friend of Cladie Bailey, and would become the Blue Jackets' coach in 1943.

Newspapers called it one of the most tragic accidents ever in Lawrence County. Few after it would be worse.

Up at the diamond, baseball no longer seemed important once the impact of the crash, that could be heard there, was known. Team members, almost in silence, began packing away the bats, the balls and the bases. There would be no game that day. Nor for the rest of the season.

The newspapers on Monday listed the victims: Homer Peters Jr., 13, son of Mr. and Mrs. Homer Peters. "Junior," his friends called him; his brother, Frank, 11, and James McArthur, 16, son of Mr. and Mrs. Leonard McArthur.

Among the injured, the papers listed Charles Kunkle, 15, and Verlin George, 18. Friends knew Charles as "Chuck" or "Charlie" and Verlin as "Froggy."

Cladie Bailey had seen each of the victims grow up, taught some of them in school, knew their parents well. He would learn of their deaths while in training at Camp Livingston.

Weeds overtook the diamond and the backstop soon collapsed, its mesh wire clinging to the posts. It later was removed and the land used for crops that would aid the war effort.

Charles Kunkle entered the Navy as soon as he was 17. He was lost at sea August 23, 1944. His grave is in Gilgal Cemetery outside Heltonville, not far from those of Junior, Frank and Jim. Verlin "Froggy" George survived his tour of duty and died at age 71 in 1993.

CHAPTER XIV

A Holiday Wedding

By then Katherine Hobson had won the heart of the bachelor. She and Bailey had decided to wed on July 4, 1941, on Cladie's first extended leave from Camp Livingston.

It was a time when civilians respected men in service, a time when elected officials were public servants. That would be important to Cladie and Katherine.

Katherine recalls the frenzied excitement of that day. "Clade couldn't get here until 10 a.m. on July 4, which meant the county clerk's office, where marriage licenses were issued, would be closed.

"I contacted Ruel Steele, the county clerk, and told him of my predicament. He said for me not to worry, that he would be over at Wilson Park, the site of the annual holiday festivities in Bedford, and he would come to the Courthouse at our convenience.

Steele, who would later become a leader in Indiana politics and state highway commissioner in the 1960s, was true to his word. He arrived at the Courthouse at noon and issued the license, then returned to the park where 15,000 people had gathered to celebrate the birth of freedom.

Katherine was as nervous as any bride. "Sam and Mildred, who had brought us together, had asked me to call them so they could meet us at the Courthouse. When Clade arrived I completely forgot about anyone else and didn't think about them until we got the license and went out to see Clade's parents. Sam and Mildred were able to meet us there."

The couple was married at 8 o'clock that night at Bloomington by Rev. Clarence Medaris at his parsonage on Morgan Street in a ceremony witnessed by Sam and Mildred. Katherine had chosen Medaris to perform the ceremony because he had been a Methodist minister at Fort Ritner southeast of Bedford where she was born.

She was 18, just out of Bedford High School. Cladie was 30, a college graduate, an officer and a gentleman. "A lot of people may have thought the 12 years difference was too much. We didn't," she said. It would not be a problem for either.

"Most men celebrate their freedom on July 4. I get to celebrate the day I lost mine," Bailey teased his bride about the date of their wedding.

"I wanted to marry someone who was mature and had a good education," Katherine recalled. Cladie filled both of those goals. He was handsome, intelligent, neat, a sharp dresser, a straight forward person. "If you asked him a question," she said, "he gave you an answer, whether you wanted that answer or not."

Miss Hobson was now Mrs. Bailey and she was leaving home for what she thought would be the last time. "I didn't think I would be back to live there," she recalled 53 years later, "but I did return," she said, her voice trailing off.

She would not be the only war bride who would return home while their husbands were at war.

One of the Bedford newspapers noted the wedding in its society columns: "Mr. and Mrs. Alva Hobson, 807 I Street, announce the marriage of their daughter, Katherine, to Lt. Cladie Bailey of Camp Livingston, Louisiana."

The new Mrs. Bailey returned with Cladie to Camp Livingston and they would be together until April 6, 1942, first there, then at Fort Benning, Ga., and later at Fort Devens, Mass.

* * *

Hoosiers, and those associated with Hoosiers, care about one another and that would be fortunate for Cladie and Katherine when they arrived as newly-weds in Alexandria, La. Apartments were difficult to find near the base where thousands of soldiers prepared for war. When Bailey responded to an advertisement for a two-room apartment, a woman answered the knock, looked at Bailey and said, "Oh, you're doctor . . . who called about the apartment."

Cladie explained he wasn't the doctor and started to leave. The woman asked where he was from. "Indiana," he replied. She

Katherine and Cladie Bailey shortly after wedding

smiled as if she had met a long-lost acquaintance, opened the door wider, invited him in and rented the apartment on the spot.

She explained she had met her husband, who was from Evansville, Ind., when he arrived at Camp Livingston for training during World War I. It was obvious she was partial to Hoosiers. Her tiny apartment would become the Bailey's first home.

When Bailey was sent that fall to Fort Benning for advanced training. the landlady rented the apartment to another couple with the firm understanding they would have to be out when the Baileys returned in three months.

The schedule at Fort Benning allowed Cladie and Katherine to plan short weekend trips which took them to Warm Springs and other places of interest.

They also were permitted to return to Indiana for the Christmas holidays. It was then, Katherine recalls, that Cladie repaid a debt to Loyd Bailey, an uncle.

Loyd had loaned Cladie some money to do graduate work at Indiana University in 1938. "I'm not sure how much it was, at least $100, but I went with him when he repaid the money. Loyd (who farmed and worked at the stone mill) had a big family (he and his wife, Edith, had raised eight children) and I know it had been a hardship for him to make the loan."

Katherine had, by then, observed Cladie as a man and as a husband. She noted that he was just as nice, polite and helpful to a bum as he was to the educated and the wealthy. "He was the same. He never varied in his kindness to people."

That holiday would be the last time Cladie Bailey would be with his family.

After three months at Fort Benning, Cladie and Katherine returned to Louisiana, awaiting transfer to Fort Devens from where, rumors said, the 32nd Division would be sent to Europe.

The unit traveled by troop train from Louisiana to Massachusetts, leaving Katherine to follow by car over narrow highways, it being an era before interstate roads. She was accompanied by another soldier's wife, who did not drive. "It was a long trip, but I didn't feel isolated because we went through so many towns. I think that made me feel safer," Katherine said.

In Massachusetts, the Baileys lived in an apartment at Ayer, a small town near Fort Devens. They knew their time together was limited and they tried to make each day longer.

CHAPTER XV

Separated by War

The men at Fort Devens had thought they would be sent to Northern Ireland as a prelude to action in Europe. They had not been at Devens long, however, when those plans changed abruptly on a fateful Sunday when the Japanese launched the sneak attack on Pearl Harbor. The day was December 7, 1941, the date President Franklin Roosevelt said would "live in infamy."

Training quickly took on an increased tempo with longer hours of work and more combat-like training. That meant Bailey would have less and less time to spend with Katherine. Soon it was learned the 32nd Division would be sent to the Pacific not across the Atlantic to Ireland.

It was a decision that would prove ominous for Bailey and the men of the 32nd Division.

It was on April 6, 1942, when Cladie called to ask Katherine to drive to the post. The division had been ordered to board a troop train en route to San Francisco from where it would depart for the South Pacific.

Katherine watched as the train faded into the distance, a 19-year-old expectant mother, unaware of what the future held, unable to change it even had she known what it was.

The Japanese had rolled through the East Indies, the Philippines, the Carolines, the Solomons and were on their way down the coast of New Guinea. Australia and New Zealand lay ahead unless the war machine from the Land of the Rising Sun was checked.

Wives of some officers departed the next day on another train, headed west to spend the final hours with their men before they went to war. Katherine decided not to make the trip. She was five months pregnant and it would be a long trip for a few short hectic days.

Decades later she would reflect on the War Department's decision to send the 32nd Division to the Pacific. "I wish it had been sent to Europe. I wish it had," she repeated softly. "He (Clade) probably would have had a better chance."

At San Francisco, the men stayed in the Cow Palace before shipping out to Australia. It was an unsettled time, but Bailey managed to keep Katherine posted on what was going on. He described, in a letter dated April 13, the scenery he had viewed from the train. "I've made up my mind that when I get back we will spend about two or three months in this part or the country. You and I and the little one," he added, continuing:

"I hope to God this is over soon so that we may be able to start where we left off, and with a little more to make life happier for us. I'm now looking forward to the day when I get off that boat for home and, wherever it is, I want you to be there to meet me."

Fate sometimes intervenes in the best of intentions.

* * *

Cladie Bailey had become known to fellow officers as "Gus," a label given him by Harry Richardson, one of his first and closest Army friends.

Richardson explained the nickname: "The Army had listed him as Cladie A. Bailey so I called him Cladie Augustus for a while. 'Gus' seemed easier to handle, so that's the way it went after a short acquaintance." Cladie would be "Gus" to fellow officers for the next four years.

To Richardson the A, which was for Alfred, had become A for Augustus, and eventually "Gus."

* * *

James I. Hunt, who would become a lawyer after the war, had met "Gus" when the officers boarded the troop train at Fort Devens.

"He was a lieutenant and I was a brand new 2nd lieutenant. Someone, probably Gus, started a poker game among the junior officers as soon as the train departed. The game lasted until we reached San Francisco. Gus was in the game all the way, but I do not remember him as a big winner or loser, but, always, as the life of the party."

Hunt, as Richardson had, soon formed a friendship with Bailey.

* * *

Francis Walden, like Bailey, was an Indiana farm boy, growing up at Stinesville, 30 miles from Heltonville.

Walden, a private, had trained at Camp Roberts in California and was sent, along with others, to San Francisco to join the 126th Infantry Regiment as a replacement. It was there he met Lieutenant Bailey, executive officer of G Company, 2nd Battalion, under Capt. Blanchard Smith, the company commander.

"We were given extra uniforms, M-1 rifles and new helmets at the Cow Palace, which was like a circus at the time. The activity never seemed to stop. There were men coming and going all the time. We slept in stalls where cows had stood during livestock expositions," Walden said.

He recalled a dock workers' strike was underway and the union refused to load the troop ship. "That work had to be done by a regular Army unit."

Despite the rigors to come, Walden managed to keep the Company G passenger list that was issued before the unit boarded the ship. He would maintain that roster for the next 50-plus years, underlining the names of officers and enlisted men as they were killed in action or when they died after the war was over.

Walden would not see Bailey as their ship crossed the Pacific but they would be reunited once the regiment landed and later would be together on one of the most grueling treks of World War II.

* * *

By then O. O. Dixon, Bailey's acquaintance from back home, was the regimental communications officer and would soon become the regimental personnel adjutant.

* * *

The 32nd Division departed San Francisco on April 22, the troop ships passing along the bay and quietly through the Golden Gate, vanishing as the sun set before them.

As a combat history of the unit would document later, the Japanese regime did not realize its conquest of the Pacific was doomed for those ships carried the men who were to be the "Heroes of Buna."

* * *

Katherine Bailey soon returned to Bedford to spend those war years with her parents.

CHAPTER XVI

Bad News From Home

Back in Heltonville, students had gathered in the assembly back on December 8, 1941, to listen over a radio as President Roosevelt spoke and Congress declared war.

America would make short work of the "Japs," some of the students, young and naive, said. In their patriotic zeal, they believed the war would be over quickly now that the U.S. was involved. Bailey would be back in a year or two to coach, some thought. Their expectations exceeded reality.

Another basketball season came and went. Loren Henderson, the top returnee from coach Bailey's 1940-41 team, was injured in a hunting accident over the Thanksgiving holiday and could play no more. Some players left to join the military service and the team finished the season with a 5-13 record.

It was not a good time for the students at the school Bailey had attended and where he had taught.

The news from both the South Pacific and Europe was not good. Talk of rationing had started. Air raid drills were ordered in case enemy bombers penetrated the U.S. coastal defense. Defense plants were on round-the-clock schedules. The war had reached the hills of southern Indiana.

On commencement night 1942, the situation worsened. The 13 seniors had marched onto the stage for the graduation ceremony that Monday in April, and listened as the Rev. J. E. Harbin gave the opening prayer, then watched as the Glee Club prepared to sing.

It was then Sally Henderson, who lived in town, ran into the gymnasium and shouted, "The school is on fire. The school is on fire."

A crowd estimated at 500 evacuated quickly and orderly as the flames moved swiftly across the roof. Men and boys salvaged what they could from the school, most of which was too engulfed to save by the time fire trucks arrived from Bedford. (The town and township had no fire department at the time.) Among the items salvaged were the basketball uniforms Bailey's players had worn.

Wood burned from the steel that formed desks, dropping onto the gymnasium as the second floor collapsed. The goals fell from the burning backboards, warped from the heat. Soon the bleachers that had been crowded with fans who had once cheered Bailey's teams were afire.

Destroyed were the original section of the school built in 1907, and the gymnasium and high school classrooms which had been added in 1925. All that remained were a few of the newer classrooms, added in 1937, and the chimney that now towered forlornly over the boiler room. Trustee Jack Clark assessed the damage at $100,000.

Firemen said the fire likely started from defective wiring in the attic, but the cause would for years be a topic for debate.

Neither the school nor the gym, because of the war, would be rebuilt for years. There would be no Heltonville basketball team during the 1942-43 season. A long hot summer and a longer, more difficult winter were ahead.

Some students whined about the conditions under which they would meet for classes, in church basements, in the Oddfellows Hall, in a store front. Would-be players griped about a season without basketball.

Had the students and fans known of the difficult struggle the men of the 126th Infantry faced they would not have complained.

They would not, however, forget coach Bailey when a new gym was finally dedicated almost a decade later.

CHAPTER XVII

An Australian Summer

The 32nd Division landed at Adelaide in South Australia in early May and went into training almost immediately. It later moved north to Brisbane, building Camp Cable between Logan Village and Tamborine. (The camp was named for Corporal Gerald O. Cable, the first member of the division killed as a result of enemy action. He had died when a Japanese submarine torpedoed the ship on which he was being transferred from Adelaide to Brisbane.)

It was there in Australia that "Gus" Bailey made more friends among officers and men. The card games continued in Australia, James Hunt recalls. "I remember one night when the lights went out and we engaged in a bull session. It was then that Gus recited 'The Cremation of Sam McGee' from beginning to end. I had never heard any Robert Service poetry before and was impressed," Hunt admitted.

A sample of that poem:

"Now Sam McGee was from Tennessee,
    where the cotton blooms and blows.
"Why he left his home in the South to roam,
    'round the Pole, God only knows.
"He was always cold, but the land of gold
    seemed to hold him like a spell;
"Though he'd often say in his homely way
    that 'he'd sooner live in hell.'

It ended with:

"There are strange things done in the midnight sun
    by the men who moil for gold;
"The Arctic trails have their secret tales
    that would make your blood run cold;
"The Northern Lights have seen queer sights,
    but the queerest they ever did see;
"Was that night on the marge of Lake LeBarge
    I cremated Sam McGee."

Harry Richardson also remembered those card games when he could easily convince Bailey to recite some of Robert Service's ballads of the Judge Bean variety about the cold North.

Bailey, he said, was "a professional at reciting from memory."

Hunt said Bailey's experience with the Civilian Conservation Corps gave him an advantage over most other lieutenants. "We all had a high regard for him and valued his comments and advice."

Another officer who valued Bailey's leadership was Herbert M. Smith, commander of the 2nd Battalion at that time. "Gus was one of the finest and most well-liked officers in the battalion. He was a junior officer during training in the U.S. and in Australia but it was evident that his leadership and mannerism had a profound bearing on Company G's training, morale and esprit de corps."

Herbert Smith would have an even higher regard for Bailey after the military campaign that was ahead.

* * *

Horace Carter adds a "Gus" tidbit from his association with Bailey in Australia:

"In Brisbane, weekends were made for captains and above. Gus was the ranking 1st lieutenant and I was the rankless 2nd lieutenant. As the highest ranking officer left in camp on those weekends, Bailey became acting battalion commander and selected me as his executive officer. He ran a light ship, making weekend camp life fun . . . no inspections, no reveille, just fun and card games."

On other occasions, higher ranking officers rode in jeeps to training areas. "Us underlings trod to and from those areas, Bailey and Carter at the head of the troops," Carter recalled.

"Gus" Bailey's reputation as a soldier's officer continued to grow.

CHAPTER XVIII

A Son is Born

Each day, back in Bedford, Ind., Katherine Bailey waited for the mail. The postman, Leonard Weaver, had told her mother, "I hate to go past your house when I don't have a letter from Clade because I see Katherine sitting there waiting for one."

The summer passed slowly as she anticipated those letters and waited for their son to be born. "We had never thought of the possibility it would be a girl," she would relate later.

They had been right. The son, Cladie Alyn, arrived on August 31 at Dunn Memorial Hospital in Bedford. Mother and son would remain there for several days, that being normal procedure at the time.

"The day I came back from the hospital with Cladie Alyn, the postman arrived with a box, a gift from Cladie, the timing a coincidence. He waited as I opened the package and found an opal ring from Australia."

The ring went on her finger immediately . . . and stayed there except when it was in a jewelry shop for repair.

A letter arrived later in which Cladie wrote that he was pleased and greatly relieved about the birth of Cladie Alyn. "I won't have to pace the tent anymore," he said.

In a short time a picture arrived, showing Cladie as he read the telegram announcing the birth of his son. In letters to come, Cladie Alyn would be referred to as "the little guy" and "our son."

Bailey's fellow officers and men under his command would hear more about "the little guy" in the years ahead for he frequently talked about his wife and son.

* * *

Katherine Bailey did not forget Cladie's parents. She had visited them often before Cladie Alyn was born, continued to make the 10-mile drive after his arrival.

War had delayed the extension of rural electric lines past the Bailey house. Katherine, who had been accustomed to electricity, soon learned there was no way to heat a formula once the fire in the kitchen range went out.

That would not cool her affection for her in-laws. "I called her Mrs. Bailey and him Jim. That may seem odd, but that's how the other girls (daughters-in-law) referred to them.

"Sometimes we girls would be talking negatively about someone and Mrs. Bailey would say, 'now girls, remember that there is a little bit of good in the worst of people and a little bit of bad in the best. You just remember that,' she would repeat.

"She didn't like us to talk about anyone. I took that to heart."

It was another admirable trait Cladie already had acquired from his parents.

PART V

CHAPTER XIX

Into Combat

Meantime, the 126 Infantry Regiment had about finished its training in Australia. It would not prepare the men well for the battle that was ahead.

The Japanese had continued their progress in New Guinea and U.S. intelligence was aware the enemy wanted to capture

Port Moresby as soon as possible. Rather than risk an amphibious landing there, the Japanese chose the Buna-Gona area on the opposite side of the peninsula.

The Territory of Papua, claimed by the British in 1884 and turned over to the Australians in 1901, was at the southeast end of New Guinea, forming what some called the tail of the bird-shaped island. The peninsula was lush with growth, a tropical area most of which remained in its natural state. The Japanese could not have picked a more dismal place to conduct a campaign, historians would conclude later.

Capture of Port Moresby, the Tokyo war makers reasoned, would give the Japanese another naval base and help cut the Allied supply line from America to Australia.

Beleaguered Australian troops fought alone against the invaders at Buna, keeping the enemy from crossing to the opposite side of the peninsula to capture Port Moresby, the capital of Papua.

The Owen Stanley Mountains separated Port Moresby and Buna. The mountains, whose peaks rise to heights of more than 13,000 feet, overshadow the entire Papuan Peninsula, running, like an immense spine, down its center to Milne Bay.

On the Buna side, the foothills of the range slope gently to the sea. The opposite side is neither gentle nor sloping. Instead, sharp ridges, razor-like in places, rise from the southwest coast, then connect with the main range to form a geographical obstacle that could, at that time, be crossed only on foot over torturous native tracks leading from one village to another.

It was into this area that part of the 32nd Division's 126th Infantry Regiment—including Cladie Bailey's G Company— would be committed to battle.

* * *

Training in jungle warfare for the 32nd Division had been brief, conducted by officers who were unfamiliar with the rigors it involved.

Lt. Gen. Robert Eichelberger, commander of I Corps to which the division was assigned, would claim later he had told General Douglas MacArthur that the men were not sufficiently trained to meet the Japanese veterans on equal terms.

Nevertheless, MacArthur, addressing the soldiers at Brisbane on September 13, 1942, announced he was sending the 32nd Division to New Guinea. Before the month was over, the division's 126th Infantry Regiment arrived by sea and went into bivouac near Port Moresby.

It was about that time that Bailey assumed command of Company G, a lieutenant in a captain's position, Blanchard Smith having left the outfit.

The arduous journey over the Owen Stanley range was about to begin.

CHAPTER XX

The Torturous Trail

Private Francis Walden, who had been under Bailey's command for four months, recalls seeing General MacArthur in Australia when the company returned from a 50-mile hike. "Once he was spotted, everyone said, 'This is it.' It wasn't long after that we got on board freighters and were on the way to Port Moresby.

"We didn't really have any training for what was ahead. All we had were a few trips out in the brush of Australia," he recalls. He also remembers that the toilet on the freighter was a wooden trough with water running through on its way into the ocean. "We had to sit on a 2-by-4 instead of a stool. When the ship got to rocking, it was difficult," he explains.

The company did not remain long in Port Moresby before being taken by trucks to a rubber plantation near a place called Kapa Kapa, where the road ended.

It was time to begin what would be a 42-day mission over the mountains along foot trails only men and beast could follow. The 172 men of Company E had started the trek a few days earlier, "the spearhead of the spearhead of the spearhead." It would soon learn it would be foolish to attempt to build a road over the maddening terrain as had been the original objective.

A member of Company E had written in his diary, "Been three weeks in New Guinea and haven't had a hot meal or a good one. I'm afraid it will become much worse than this."

It would be no easier for Bailey or the men of Company G, who would follow.

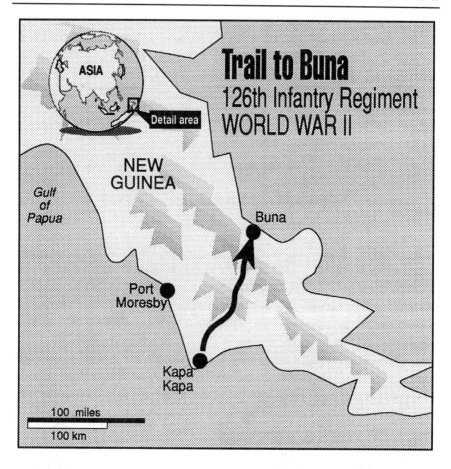

Walden, lets the video of the mind rewind to those days, then plays them back. "We had no pack animals, unless you considered us pack animals. We just had ourselves. We had no change of clothes. Once in a while when we got muddy we'd just jump into a stream and wash what we had on. That water was cold coming down out of the mountains. I mean it was cold."

Life for Bailey and the other company officers was no better.

Walden recalls, "Bailey usually led a column along the trail and another officer would bring up a column from behind. We were strung out single file a long way because the trail was so narrow, which meant I usually only saw Lieutenant Bailey at night."

Walden recalls one night on the rugged trail when his company commander greeted him as the company bivouacked.

"Lieutenant Bailey hollered at me and said, 'Come here, Walden. I want to know where you are from in Indiana.' I said 'from Stinesville, sir.' He laughed and said, 'My, gosh!,' and then reminded me that he had taken some of his Heltonville teams to play at Stinesville. He laughed, and said, 'When we beat you guys we had to get out of town in a hurry or we'd get beat up.' "

Bailey never forgot he was from a small Indiana town, no matter where fate took him. And no matter how many promotions he would receive, he never considered himself above the men in his command.

Walden lets his memories return to the trail: "We slept in pup tents at night and we'd sometimes cut branches off trees and sleep on them to keep off the wet bare ground. We often ran short of food. Usually for breakfast we had corn beef, a half can each for two men. At night we might get five or six spoonsful of rice. When we went across the main ridge, we had to carry enough food for five days. It wouldn't have lasted most people more than two days."

When supply planes were unable to locate the company for several days, Colonel Lawrence A. Quinn, the regimental commander, decided on November 5 to make the flight, hoping to observe the situation and possibly offer some assistance in selecting locations for parachute drops.

Once Company G was located near a place called Natunga, the men aboard the plane kicked out a box of supplies. The parachute opened too quickly and part of its cord wrapped around the tail of the plane, causing it to crash in view of the men of the company. Everyone aboard, including Colonel Quinn, was killed.

It was obvious to the soldiers of Company G who viewed the wreckage that war is indeed a misadventure. Tragedy, however, can be only a temporary setback and the men continued their laborious journey.

Walden returns to the trail: "There was one place we went down that was like a slide. The soil was gone and the surface was almost entirely stone. We had to almost get on our hands and knees and crawl down. It was almost as if the trail had disappeared.

"I don't recall how many miles we went each day, but it wasn't very many. We did finally get new shoes from air drops because the ones we started out with were about to rot off our feet. The new boots had slick soles which made it difficult to stand up.

"It was hot and humid most of the time, except on the very top of the mountain where we could see our breath. We were wet most of the time. I think the day we went over the top of the mountain it rained for 18 straight hours . . . not hard, just a slow drizzle.

"We had to build a fire every night to cook the rice. Trying to start a fire with wet wood wasn't easy. We had to peel the bark off white trees that looked something like our sycamores to get the wood to burn. Then a couple of guys would hold a raincoat over two other soldiers who would use mosquito repellent to start a fire. Our matches were usually wet so we had to find a dry spot on our uniform, then rub the heads of the matches real easy until they were dry enough to strike."

Walden recalls that most of the men grew weak from diarrhea and hunger during the torturous march. "The officers went through the same things we did. They were right there with us. They had to do their own cooking, too."

It was a rare opportunity for enlisted men to observe their officers. "To all us guys, Bailey was No. 1. I mean he was an all-round good man. You couldn't ask for a better officer or a better man. He was sort of just one of the guys. Some officers, you know, seemed stuck up, acted like they didn't want to be bothered with enlisted men. That didn't make any difference to Bailey. He was right there with us. That's what I liked about him."

* * *

One of the officers on the trail with Bailey and his men was 2nd Lieutenant Harry Williams, a young New York Life insurance agent from Chester, S. C.

Williams had met Bailey at Camp Livingston, La., upon being assigned to the unit in February, 1942, as a reserve officer.

Still an agent for New York Life, he remembers the rigors of the Owen Stanley crossing. "Will, of course, all my life," he adds.

"As the crow flies, I believe it was 125 miles from Port Moresby to Buna. But we walked a lot further than that going up and down all the time, so I'm sure we covered twice that distance. As I recall, we got up as high as 9,500 or 10,000 feet. I think that was the general opinion. But we really didn't know how high we were."

Williams recalled that Bailey never lost his sense of humor, not even on that long mountain traipse. "He had a lot of funny sayings. He was witty and you didn't have to be around him long before you were laughing, too. One of the funny things he said one time . . . maybe when he was getting everybody up back in Australia . . . was, 'Most people die in bed. Get up! Get up!' "

His comment, unfortunately, would be more prophetic than he would ever know.

"Gus was a great fellow, a wonderful guy. Everybody loved him," Williams added.

CHAPTER XXI
Battle of Buna

Company G and the rest of the battalion eventually made its way past Natunga, through Gora and then to Bofu on November 12, 1942. By November 21, Major Smith's 2nd Battalion, which included Bailey's Company G, had arrived at Soputa.

The men trod into the Buna front, the Division's history records, with weapons and ammunition, cups and spoons, and the tattered, sweat-stained, mold-stinking battle dress which they had worn since leaving Port Moresby.

"Extra clothing, shoes, personal belongings, and even essentials, the very weight of which made them non-essentials to the men who had to carry them, were dropped in salvage dumps along the trail."

Lieutenant Bailey would write to his wife that the men had diarrhea so bad he sometimes had to carry his pack and those of two or three men.

Company G had met no resistance on the trail, but that was to change.

* * *

War is not always fair and that was never more obvious than to the men of Major Herbert Smith's 2nd Battalion, 126th Infantry, which included Lieutenant Bailey's company. They had endured an arduous mission, tromped through mud, gone hungry and dirty, lived on hope, rice and wild bananas for six weeks.

Yet, the 1st and 3rd Battalions had been flown over the mountains, a short journey by air, after it was learned there was a usable airfield near Buna.

The 2nd Battalion, including Bailey's men, in need of rest after its march over the mountains, was to remain in the Soputa area in reserve, to be called on when needed during the battle of Buna.

The 32nd Division went into its first action with many of its men already short of rations and weakened by sickness. It lacked ample engineering equipment or medical supplies and the men had no experience in jungle warfare.

Nevertheless, the Allied advance units reached the outposts of the Japanese position at Buna on November 18. The book, "World War II," reports:

"The next morning they attacked and immediately found themselves halted by heavy fire from an unseen enemy. Allied infantry—armed only with rifles, grenades, and machine guns, and supported by a few mortars and pieces of artillery—were thrust against a strong, carefully prepared defensive system. Radio equipment proved unreliable; losses and sickness mounted; morale sagged."

It was to be a short rest for Bailey's company and the rest of the 2nd Battalion. It had no sooner settled itself in its bivouac area than it was ordered back over the Giruwa River to rejoin the 32nd Division on November 22. The river was flooded and it was obvious the men could not ford the stream, which seemed to Francis Walden to be two or three times as wide as Indiana's White River.

He recalls that someone swam across the river and tied a cable which he had taken to the opposite side. The men then crossed in rafts using the cable as a guide in the darkness.

The first action Company G saw, as Francis Walden recalls, was on December 1, 1942, but adds, "Time didn't mean much then."

It is Walden's recollection that three men in Company G—Private Paul Allen, Private First Class John Kitchka and Sergeant Louis Vander Hoeven—were killed that day.

"I know I got hit on December 5 by a sniper. I had a Thompson submachine gun in my hand and the bullet went through the stock, into my hand and out, burning a streak along my arm as it went past. I was taken to a hospital from where I was evacuated the next day. A day later, December 7, 1942 (a date that indeed was living in infamy), the Japanese blew the hospital to pieces."

Company G continued to fight on.

Time can erode memories and Harry Williams' recollection of the first action is slightly different than Francis Walden's. "We were going through a trail lined with brown Kunai grass which was about four feet high. We pulled off at a level place along the trail, stopped and laid down flat in the area next to that high grass. I was down when I decided I'd better check our rear position. I looked back and saw two men, 30 yards to the rear. They had raised up in the grass behind us and I yelled, 'Japs,' as I jumped and rolled into the Kunai grass. So did the other men. The Japs fired and hit the guy in front of me. As I recall it was Sergeant Leonard Fionda who was killed."

Williams adds, thoughtfully: "It was the first casualty our company had that I know of. It could have been me, it could have been anyone. You never understand why one person is hit and another is not."

It would be the first of many casualties Company G would experience in the next few weeks. Lieutenant Williams would be the only officer of Company G who would fly out of Buna once the battle was won. Only nine enlisted men who were with the unit from the start would be with him.

* * *

The fighting at Buna raged on. On December 2, according to the book, "Victory in Papua," Company G was on the western end of what was called the strip. "Led by its commander, 1st Lieutenant Cladie A. Bailey, it overran strong enemy opposition on its part of the strip."

For that night's action, Cladie Bailey would later receive the Distinguished Service Cross, the second highest military honor a soldier can receive.

The unit had overrun enemy shelling and machine gun replacements and mopped up a hostile bivouac position. Bailey then advanced with his company to a position where it could cover the flank of the attack force.

Hours passed, progress was slow. The attack seemed stalled on December 5. Then came what the book "Victory in Papua" called "electrifying news" from Lieutenant Bailey. Staff Sergeant Herman J. F. Bottcher, who headed a platoon from Company H that had been assigned to Bailey's company, had pushed north, knocking out pillboxes en route. Bottcher had crossed a creek under enemy fire and by late afternoon had reached the breech with 18 men and one machine gun.

Bottcher, who had served with the Loyalists in the Spanish Civil War, used the machine gun to eliminate the enemy. Bottcher would receive a battlefield commission and the Distinguished Service Cross for his heroism, but he would not survive the war to enjoy his goal of becoming a U.S. citizen.

The battle was far from won. The enemy line was too strong for a frontal attack on Buna Village. Fighting went on, the 2nd Battalion of the 126th Infantry involved, it seemed, almost daily until Allied reinforcements arrived and B-25 bombers dropped demolitions on the village.

Bailey was wounded on December 19 and eventually would be flown back to Australia. The Battle of Buna ended in January, an Allied victory that had not come easily or cheaply.

Bailey's Company G's strength when the 126th Infantry was returned to Port Moresby consisted of one officer, Lieutenant Harry Williams, and 27 enlisted men, some of whom had been replacements. It had departed for battle with seven or eight times that number.

There had been 8,546 American and Australian casualties in the fighting at Buna. The Japanese, it is estimated, had 13,000 to 15,000. Another 2,334 Americans were disabled by disease.

It had been a costly victory, but an important one. "It was at Buna," as the division history records, "that General MacArthur started his return to the Philippines. It was at Buna that the 32nd Division helped win the first U.S. Army ground campaign against the Japanese."

* * *

O. O. Dixon, who was a captain at the time and S-3 (operations officer) for the regimental commander, had no contact with Bailey in the Buna campaign. Dixon, who later would become a colonel and a career officer, assessed the campaign:

"We (the division) didn't have a chance. The Japanese had dug trenches and covered them over. They would run from one end of the trench to the other and we had no idea whether we were fighting 15, 30 or maybe a hundred men. The regiment had only one battery of artillery to support it and every round that was fired had to be carried on the back of a mule, one round one mule. If you wanted artillery fire on Thursday you had to order it on Tuesday. You didn't have the accuracy you needed with mortar.

"We didn't beat the Japs. We denied them supplies. They starved out. One morning they were just gone, he recalls."

* * *

Francis Walden next saw Bailey back at Port Moresby. "I was in the shower, and Bailey walked in so we talked while he showered. I asked him if he was a captain yet, and he said, 'I don't know.' I was almost sure he was, but he didn't brag about it. He was an officer, but he remained just one of the men."

Bailey had written in a journal each day the names of the men who had been killed. When the company was returned to Australia, he wrote letters to the nearest of kin of the dead. As the company orderly, it was Walden's job to type those 29 letters for Bailey's signature.

CHAPTER XXII

Initiative and Courage

It was in Australia where Bailey and others received their DSC medals. His recognition stated that as commander of a rifle company, he had led an assault without regard for personal safety, inspiring his command by his example of initiative and courage.

James Hunt, who had been communications officer at battalion headquarters, was wounded at Buna before Bailey and also had earned the Distinguished Service Cross.

The medals were presented to Hunt, Bailey and others cited for bravery in the first Allied land offensive in the Pacific by General Eichelberger at Camp Cable.

Hunt remembers, "We (he and Bailey) were side by side while the general pinned the medals to our uniforms, and of course, we stood ramrod straight at attention. In an interlude before the troops passed in review, Gus asked for help because the general had pinned his medal to the skin. It had drawn blood, but Gus never flinched."

About that time, Bailey was promoted to captain and soon given command of the 1st Battalion, 126th Infantry Regiment, 32nd Division.

Bailey and Hunt would renew their friendship from time to time as the war continued.

* * *

Francis Walden retained a copy of a program handed to men who on March 28, 1943, attended a memorial service for soldiers of the regiment who had been killed in action in New Guinea from September, 1942, to January, 1943. Seventeen of the men were from Bailey's Company G, killed after surviving that 42-day march over the mountains.

* * *

Bailey had his first opportunity in two months to write to Katherine on Christmas Day, December 25, 1942. He did not mention the Distinguished Service Cross he had won.

With pen, he explained: "I am in a hospital somewhere in Australia. Nothing to worry about. The American Red Cross gave us a large box with candy, gum, mints etc., last evening and when I awakened this morning there was a stocking at the foot of my bed with an orange, banana, candy and gum. Makes us feel pretty good."

He asked that she thank the Red Cross through the newspaper at home.

"Sometime ago I received 17 letters in one mail delivery. Among them I found three pictures of our child and I sure was overjoyed to get them. Of course everyone had to take a look.

"Soon the little one will be four months old. He must be growing fast. I am looking forward to the day when I can walk down that gangway to home," Captain Bailey wrote.

He mentioned, almost as an aside, that he had been recommended for captain and that O. O. Dixon had been recommended for major.

The Bedford Times-Mail, a merger of the two county seat papers back home, printed a picture of Bailey with the announcement of his DSC award and the promotion to captain.

"He has an unusual treat in store when he returns—his first sight of his son born four months ago," the caption under his picture read. Not even newspapers can forecast the future.

It was about that time that Bailey talked with Katherine over a radio hook up. The connection was bad and conversation was difficult.

Katherine would continue to share her letters with her in-laws, especially Mamie who by then was also her confidant and her friend.

* * *

Herbert Smith, who had been commander of the 2nd Battalion at Buna, called Bailey "one of the finest and most well-liked officers in the battalion. Gus was a down-to-earth individual, took a practical view of any situation and through adversity or victory he displayed the highest standards of leadership. He never lost the twinkle in his eyes, the ready smile or cheerful greeting."

PART VI

CHAPTER XXIII
Rest and Regroup

Back in Australia, Bailey continued to make new friends as the 126th Infantry Regiment was rebuilt and retrained so it would be better prepared to meet the enemy in its next engagement.

It would be an interlude from battle, a time when he and Harry Richardson would become even closer companions.

After Bailey was released from the hospital, he and Richardson went on a nine-day leave to Sydney. "We rounded up the dress uniforms which we had tailored in Brisbane on our first arrival at Camp Cable. Gus said it never rained in Sydney, so we left our raincoats behind and endured nine days of rain. He (Gus) had many accomplishments to his credit, but I never let him forget that weather forecasting was not one of them.

"While in Sydney, between the rain, we went to the race track to see the horses run. The humor of being novices at the sport was something we would talk about later over cribbage games. Gus did come up with one gem by the name of Eureka (which coincidentally was the name of a tiny community back home in Lawrence County). I can still hear him calling on old Eureka to win. The horse did finish first and Gus came out well financially. Perhaps, the stop at the bar first helped increase our yelling ability that encouraged Eureka to move out front to stay."

Bailey and Richardson would continue to see each other despite the island-jumping to come. They would grow even closer in a relationship related descriptively by Richardson:

"I suppose we never quite know what draws men together in matters of friendship. When I think of Gus as a friend it's not so much as if our backgrounds were the same but we were bound up in a struggle to keep our nation free. I'll say that I admired Gus as a great warrior and many others will verify that he was indeed that. Because of that fact, I'm sure he helped me and others over some rough times."

* * *

General William H. Gill assumed command of the 32nd Division early in 1943. In 1953, looking back 10 years, Gill wrote: "The troops had taken part in the Papuan campaign and were in bad shape. I think somewhere in the records it will be shown that almost 8,000 had malaria, certainly the morale of officers and men was low. The troops had to be cured in body and mind before any effective training for renewed combat could be accomplished."

Bailey's 1st Battalion would spend the next eight months preparing for its second encounter of the war.

In the meantime Bailey would continue to cement his associations not only with Harry Richardson, but with Don Ryan, Sol Jaffe, Russell Gonsoulin, Lloyd Fish, Oliver Dixon, Eugene Frost, James Hunt, Elmer Geik, William Chapman, Horace Carter and other officers.

They had been brought together by a war they had not started. Together they would help bring it to an end.

* * *

It was about that time that Don Ryan was assigned to the 1st Battalion where Bailey had been transferred as the operations officer.

"When I joined the division as a replacement second lieutenant in January, 1943, Bailey was a captain. The division spent some time in recuperation on the coast, then returned to Camp Cable.

"My first experience with Bailey came when we were in Newcastle, Australia, taking amphibious training. I had been an enlisted man before going to OCS where I was commissioned in November, 1942. As a sergeant, I had gone through radio and communications training so I was a halfway decent radio operator.

"I was assigned to the 1st Battalion as a communications officer. At Fort Stevens near Newcastle, a Lt. Col. Marvin, an old timer from WWI and the battalion commander, was making the rounds of our exercise area with Captain Bailey. Marvin spotted me sitting at one of the radio sets fiddling with the dials. He turned to Bailey and said, 'What in the heck is Ryan doing operating a radio?'

"Bailey replied, 'Well, he's probably showing the enlisted men now to calibrate the set.' That was exactly what I was doing. Bailey had come right to my defense . . . and I appreciated that."

It was another example of Bailey's support of the men in his units.

* * *

Lloyd B. Fish joined the 32nd in late February when the division was beginning to regroup, being "fleshed out" as Fish called it, with draftees, new ROTC officers and "recent 2nd lieutenant graduates of 'the Benning School for Boys' at Fort Benning" (Fish's name for Officers Candidate School).

Fish soon observed that Bailey's combat experience in Buna put him on top of the situation as the battalion operations and training officer.

That experience allowed Captain Bailey and other veteran officers to earn the trust and respect of subordinates. That experience would allow those leaders to display their competence as the regiment moved up through the islands later.

In a few months, Bailey "volunteered" Fish, who was a company platoon leader at the time, for a division intelligence training course. "I didn't realize that Bailey's approach to combat intelligence was that you had to go out and get it. It would not come to you.

"Soon after the course was over, Bailey appointed me battalion S-2 (intelligence officer). Little did I realize that his decision would set me on a career path in military intelligence that I would follow throughout the remainder of my military service."

He adds wistfully: "I regret I never had the opportunity to express my appreciation and gratitude for this and other major decisions Bailey made in my behalf."

CHAPTER XXIV

Return to Combat

That spring and summer would prepare the 32nd Division for battles to come. When the time came to fight again, it was better equipped, better trained, ready to drive the Japanese back toward the islands from which they had come.

By then, Captain Bailey had become commander of the 1st Battalion and on October 15 would be promoted to major. No one was happier about those two developments than the officers and men he would lead.

Don Ryan explains: "We felt very comfortable with Bailey. For one thing you could talk to him. He would listen to you and I never saw him lose his cool the whole time we were together. If I had some ideas about how to do something, he would listen to me."

He gave his officers and men confidence in themselves and in their commanders.

The division had moved north in September, 1943, to Milne Bay then to Goodenough Island for additional jungle training. It was about to re-enter combat.

* * *

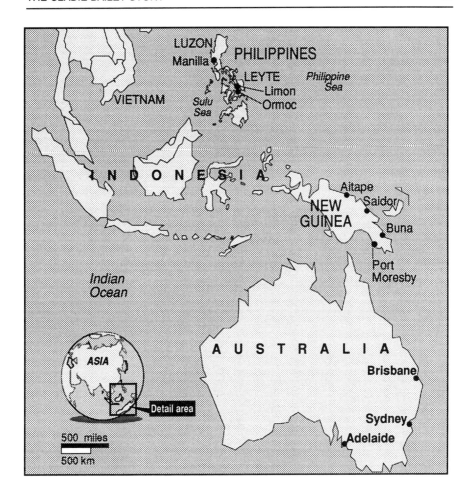

Don Ryan recalls that en route to Milne Bay, he was offered a fifth of VAT 69 for 10 pounds, or about $32, by a crewman aboard the Australian ship HMAS Duntroon.

"I thought what the hell, I might just as well, so I bought it even though some other lieutenants said it was crazy to pay that kind of money for a fifth of Scotch. I figured we might have a little party before we went into action.

"On Christmas Eve at Goodenough Island we were aware we were going into combat at Saidor within a week. I decided, heck, this is a good time to have the Scotch, so we brought the officers together. It just happened that one of my extra duties was to be the mess officer, which allowed me to talk the mess sergeant out of a couple of cans of juice. I gave him in return a bottle of Gilbey's gin I had brought from Australia and he handed me two extra apple pies he had baked for the following day.

"One of the other officers talked the orderly for Colonel Joseph Bradley, the regimental commander, out of ice cubes made in the regiment's only refrigerator, which was run by kerosene.

"We wound up with a good group of officers in the tent, and we did a good job on the bottle of Scotch. All the lieutenants of the company, plus the executive officer, were there. It was a great evening, except for the fact Major Bailey was missing.

"The next morning before breakfast Bailey walked by the tent. He said, 'Geez, I hear you guys had a party last night.'

"I said we did, and told him we had looked for him."

It was then Bailey explained, "I was over with the regimental commander, but he didn't have a heck of a lot to drink. And on top of that he didn't have any ice cubes."

The other officers laughed, knowing where the ice cubes had gone. Bailey then asked, "I don't suppose you saved any of that VAT 69 for me?"

Ryan lied, "I'm sorry. We emptied that whole bottle."

"Major Bailey," Ryan related, "looked kind of crestfallen and I started to laugh. I then went into the tent and came out with the bottle which still held a drink we had saved for him. You should have seen his face light up. He drank that and off we went to breakfast."

* * *

On January 2, 1944, the 1st Battalion joined in an amphibious assault at Saidor, New Guinea.

Like the area between Port Moresby and Buna, Saidor was surrounded by high mountains and swamp-bordered streams. There were no roads and thick, tropical growths covered much of the area. Most histories indicate the 1st Battalion saw little combat there. Lloyd Fish and Don Ryan disagree. Fish explains:

"Both the Saidor operation and the one to come at Aitape, although initially lightly opposed on the beaches, developed into extensive sharp and decisive confrontations with a regrouped and reinforced Japanese military. In each operation the battalion was committed to long range aggressive patrols deep inland into the mountains and along the coastal plains. These patrols made numerous hostile encounters and suffered considerable casualties. Major Bailey not only directed these operations; he went out to make sure they were properly executed."

Don Ryan remembers: "We had moved directly to an area where our engineers were to build an airfield. We then set up a headquarters on an island in the middle of the Mot River from where we sent a platoon, finally a company, then more reinforcements to pursue the Japanese who were on the other side of the river.

"As I recall, Bailey went right across the river with the attacking forces. He didn't return until things finally settled down."

It was further evidence that Bailey did not send his men where he would not go himself.

* * *

Shortly before the Mot River operation, the 126th Infantry was visited by Lt. Gen. Walter Kreuger, commanding general of the 6th Army, who wanted to know how long it had been since the men had been served fresh meat.

The mess sergeant tried to equivocate, causing the general to exclaim, "Don't try to kid me. I used to be a mess officer myself." He was then told it had been a couple of months since meat had been available.

"Make a note of that," General Kreuger said to his aid.

Within two or three days, C-47 transports loaded with fresh beef, apparently from Australia, landed in the mud at the airfield the Japanese had tried unsuccessfully to develop before fleeing.

* * *

Major O. O. Dixon commanded the 2nd Battalion when the 126th Infantry went into Saidor. That meant both the 1st and

2nd Battalions were led by men who had grown up back in Lawrence County, Indiana, still friendly rivals in enemy territory. It was a coincidence that likely was not repeated elsewhere in the war.

Bailey and Dixon, of course, were brought together each time the regimental commander called a meeting. Dixon recalls one incident that occurred during the second New Guinea campaign after the Japanese had been routed into the hills.

"My battalion was chosen to make an independent amphibious operation up the coast where the Japanese were coming down out of the hills. We got on boats about 2 a.m. and landed at daybreak the next day. At the same time, Bailey's battalion had been given a mission to proceed by foot up the coast in case there were any Japs in between, then meet us. Bailey wanted to get up there and take my objective before I arrived.

"I remember that he kidded me about almost being able to reach the destination (on foot) before we did."

* * *

It was about that time that Brig. Gen. Robert Martin, the assistant division commander, arrived for a visit, which would result in another anecdote, this one also involving beef.

One of the men in the battalion had, against regulations, shot a cow roaming in the area. The staff surgeon inspected the animal and declared it safe for consumption. It was butchered and cooked for dinner, which was the noon meal in the Army.

Ryan recalls, "General Martin joined us, but made no mention of the steak even though he knew full well we had no access to government-issued fresh beef in that area. When he finished, he asked to see the day's menu, which listed the main dinner course as Australian bully beef that came in a can. I thought, 'Oh! Oh!' we're in trouble.' Instead the general turned to Major Bailey and said, 'My compliments to the chef. He really knows how to disguise that bully beef.' I was relieved . . . and I think Bailey was, too."

Sol Jaffe remembers when four natives arrived at the battalion headquarters carrying a giant turtle stretched over two poles. Turtle eggs and turtle soup were soon on the menu.

CHAPTER XXV
Advance to Aitape

The division's next objective was to secure the Hollandia region of Netherlands New Guinea. In April, 1944, the 1st Battalion moved toward Aitape, which had been occupied by the Japanese in late 1942. The entire region was a coastal plain, varying from five to thirteen miles in width, swampy in many places and cut by numerous streams.

To make matters worse, April marked the end of the wettest season in the region where rainfall averages about 100 inches per year.

Intelligence reports indicated that the Japanese ground defenses in the Aitape area were weak. It was assumed there would be little opposition to a land attack and the assault force, once ashore, could quickly seize the air strip area.

It was at that time, May 15, 1944, that Bailey was promoted to lieutenant colonel. He had been a major exactly six months.

Bailey's 1st Battalion and other units of the 32nd Division were assigned to the perimeter along the Driniumor River near Aitape. Later that month, the 1st Battalion was ordered to cross the river and head east to a village called Yakamul.

Ryan recalls, "We did get into some skirmishes with some forward elements the Japanese had sent out from Wewak. After a couple of days, division ordered us—Colonel Bailey that is—to take a company at least, plus elements from support groups and communications, and move inland several miles to a place called Afua. I decided I would go with them. They got into a skirmish in there and it didn't amount to a heck of a lot."

One incident Ryan recreated involved the Driniumor River. "We had moved out at night in the pitch black jungle and there was a Piper Cub flying over head to guide us along the trail. The river was too deep to cross and we had to wade downstream, holding our weapons and equipment above our heads while trying to avoid limbs that stuck out over the water. Believe it or not, there were crocodiles in that river. Fortunately they didn't bother us."

In another engagement, Bailey's battalion ran into strong resistance east of Yakamul on May 31. The battalion's experiences the next few days are described in the book, "Approach to the Philippines."

"During the night of June 1, Japanese artillery shelled the battalion command post. The next morning the battalion was divided into two parts. One group was put under the command of Captain Gile A. Herrick and designated Herrick Force. The rest of the Battalion, called Bailey Force, moved south down the trail from Yakamul to patrol along the Harech River.

"On June 3 the enemy launched a series of minor attacks against Company A, which was separated from the rest of Herrick Force by a small unbridged stream about four feet deep and varying in width from 10 to 50 yards. Under cover of these attacks, other Japanese groups bypassed Herrick Force to the south and the next morning appeared west of Yakamul, between Herrick Force and the perimeter of Company G of the 127th Infantry.

"Because Company A was in danger of being surrounded, Captain Herrick ordered the unit to withdraw across the small stream to Yakamul. During the movement the Japanese continued to attack, and toward the end of the hour, succeeded in overrunning some of Company A's automatic weapons positions. Deprived of this support, most of the remaining troops retreated rapidly across the stream, leaving behind radios, mortars, machine guns and 20 to 25 dead and wounded men. Most of the wounded managed to cross the stream after dark.

"When he learned of the situation at Yakamul, General Martin ordered Bailey Force to return to the coast and relieve Herrick Force. Radio communication difficulties delayed the message, forcing Bailey to organize his force in the darkness of the heavy jungle. By that time the Japanese had a strong force blocking the trail to Yakamul. After an arduous overland march through trackless, heavy jungle terrain, the leading elements of Bailey Force began straggling into Company G's perimeter about noon the next day.

"General Martin then ordered Bailey Force to move east and drive the Japanese from the Yakamul area, but changed the order when he learned the men had marched for over 13 hours on empty stomachs and were not yet completely assembled at Company G's perimeter. The men in Bailey Force ate from Company G's limited food supply, then went west along the coastal trail to the Driniumor River. Company G and the battery of the 126th Field Artillery Battalion which it had been protecting moved back to the Driniumor late in the afternoon.

"Meanwhile, the evacuation of Herrick Force from Yakamul had also been ordered and on June 5 small boats arrived at Yakamul from Blue Beach to pick up the beleaguered troops. Insofar as time permitted, radios, ammunition and heavy weapons for which there was no room on the boats were destroyed. As this work was under way, a few light mortar and light machine guns kept up a steady fire on the Japanese who, now surrounding the entire perimeter, had been harassing Herrick Force since dawn. At the last possible moment, just when it seemed the Japanese were about to launch a final infantry assault, Captain Herrick ordered his men to make for the small boats on the run. The move was covered by friendly rocket and machine gun fire from an LCM standing off shore. So fast and well organized was the sudden race for the boats, that the Japanese had no time to get all their weapons into action, and only one American was wounded during the boarding.

"The small craft hurriedly left the area and took Herrick Force to Blue Beach, where the unit was re-equipped. In a few hours the troops rejoined the rest of the 1st Battalion on the Driniumor River."

Eventually the Japanese would be routed and the bodies of the dead Americans would be recovered.

The Battalion's losses during the Driniumor River operation were 18 killed and 75 wounded. Japanese losses were much heavier.

Sol Jaffe, who had joined the 1st Battalion in 1943 as a lieutenant just out of Officers Candidate School, remembers the Driniumor River action:

"It was at Aitape that Bailey showed exceptional command ability by leading the battalion on a combat scouting mission up the river where he flushed out the Japanese forces who were trying to break out of the entrapment. The Japs were unable to break through our defenses, losing hundreds of men in an attempt to attack our machine gun positions.

"Colonel Bailey's ability as a combat leader was obvious in that operation. Every man under his command had the highest respect for him."

Jaffe cites an example of Bailey's support of his men. "An assistant to the general reported that the men in the battalion would be sent a statement of charges for the weapons abandoned when they departed Yakamul. Colonel Bailey insisted that men were not to be charged for the loss of equipment in battle. The general agreed."

* * *

The Japanese 18th Army would lose 9,300 men in the Aitape operation. Seven of its nine regiments were destroyed.

The 32nd Division history records that "out-maneuvered at every turn and relentlessly pounded by artillery fire, the remnants of the 18th Army retreated towards Wewak. The Japanese army had been destroyed . . . in a battle of maneuvers through the most dense tropical jungles. Hollandia was never threatened."

It had not been an easy Allied victory. In all, 11 of its battalions had been involved in the operation, often surviving on rations and equipment dropped by C-47 cargo planes.

General MacArthur again called on the 32nd Division, this time to move to Morotai, a tiny coral island midway between New Guinea and the southern Philippines. He was sure by then he would fulfill his "I shall return" promise.

* * *

Once the Aitape operation was successful, Corporal Francis Walden, who had remained with the 2nd Battalion after Bailey had been transferred to the 1st, was preparing to return to the States, his tour over.

"Colonel Bailey was having a staff meeting when he saw me. He stopped the meeting, called me over to his tent and we talked while the other officers waited. They probably thought I was awful because I hadn't saluted.

"He told me to let people back in Indiana know that we were still in a hell hole, or something like that."

Walden still wonders how many other officers would have delayed a staff meeting to talk with an enlisted man.

It was the last time Walden would see Bailey, but he would remember his commander's kindness and respect for his men for decades to come.

* * *

On September 15, 1944, the 126th Infantry Regiment landed on Morotai. "We were about 12 miles from the island of Halmehera where the Japanese were stationed. We could look over and see the island from where they flew night bombing raids on us," Don Ryan recalls. "They would also send troops over by barge at night, so it was a running fight for a while."

It was, however, a respite for the unit, which was detailed in groups to unload ships. The war, however, for the 126th Infantry Regiment and its 1st Battalion was far from over.

PART VII

CHAPTER XXVI
A Word of Caution

Although Colonel Bailey wrote to his wife and his parents as often as possible, he told them little about the action he saw. Except for news stories, they had no way of following the 32nd Division as it moved north from Australia into New Guinea, onto Morotai and eventually to the Philippines.

"Sometimes I would get three letters a week, sometimes none," Katherine recalls. About all Bailey could tell her, or his parents, was that he was "island hopping in the Pacific."

"There were times," Katherine remembers, "when I'd visit Mrs. Bailey and we'd get to talking and telling each other about what was in our letters. She would fix lunch, but we really didn't feel hungry. We knew he might not have food."

Rationing was not a problem for war wives such as Katherine. The shortage of shoes, sugar, tires, gasoline and other items did not seem as important to them as their concerns over their husbands' welfare.

Katherine remembers well one letter she wrote, and the answer she received. Some field officers, she knew, stayed behind the action, let others lead men into battle. She had heard from wives of other officers that Bailey was often out front with his battalion.

In that letter Katherine reminded Bailey that he was now a family man. "You stay back. I want you to come home and help raise this little boy," she wrote.

Bailey, indeed was a family man. But he was also a patriot. His reply was both gentle and firm. "Don't ever write like that again," he pleaded. "I will not send the boys anywhere I will not go myself."

CHAPTER XXVII

The Battle for Leyte

General MacArthur and his staff had decided to bypass other islands and invade Leyte, one of the southern Philippines. Eager to pursue the enemy, he pushed up the invasion date from December 20 to October 20, 1944.

The combat-experienced 126th Regiment was held in reserve, Don Ryan explains, and did not make the original assault.

"We (the 1st Battalion and the 32nd Division) went in about A-plus 10 and eventually moved up to a place called Pinamapoon where we relieved the 24th Division, which had made the initial landing."

The 24th Division had captured Breakneck Ridge a second time by November 14 and prepared to do its part to destroy the enemy forces on the west coast of Leyte. Meantime, however, the Japanese had managed to get another division ashore near Ormoc.

It was then when the 32nd Division arrived to give added momentum to the offensive and relieve the tired troops of the 24th Division who had been in action for over three weeks.

Lloyd Fish, who had rejoined Bailey's battalion after recovering from yellow jaundice, relates what followed:

Lloyd Fish

Don Ryan

"The 1st Battalion was committed in the drive south, flanking the highway from Carrigara to Ormoc. We moved through a region of heavily forested mountains and high overgrown ridges. There was considerable Japanese opposition.

"This was a brutal operation; there were no roads, only primitive native trails. It rained almost all the time. The trails to the rear were so mud-slick and hazardous that our supply lines for rations, ammunition and evacuation of the sick and wounded were totally inadequate much of the time.

"The only available zones for air drops were in valleys and then only when the clouds and fogs lifted. And then it was questionable who would be in the drop area first, our ration parties or the Japanese stragglers behind our lines. In several instances the battalion ration carriers really did fight for our supper."

Colonel Bailey by then had gained a reputation as an officer who would listen to his men. Don Ryan, who was the battalion communications officer, had convinced Bailey that the unit would be better off if it used light weight wire (W-130) instead of the regular heavy wire (W-110).

That allowed one man to carry a one-mile spool of wire whereas it had taken two men to unroll a half-mile line of the heavier wire. As a result, the battalion could carry 8 to 10 miles of wire as it moved forward.

"I told Bailey the Japs could cut the heavy wire as easily as they could the light wire and that we could extend our communications line a lot farther by being able to carry more wire," Ryan explained.

"We moved behind the Japanese lines at Limon and, I found out later, we were the only battalion in the regiment that had communications throughout the campaign."

Colonel Bailey had once again valued the opinion of another officer . . . and seen it pay off.

* * *

Lack of food, damp weather and terrain hampered the regiment's operation. So did fragments of Japanese units, split off from their units, who moved throughout the area.

All those factors, Lloyd Fish explains, made the operation "a slow, tedious, frustrating process."

Don Ryan recalls one incident. "En route to a hill, we ran into a sniper strapped up in a tree. He was covering a point where a giant tree had fallen across the trail. Colonel Bailey was standing on the near side of the tree, telling the men to hurry so the sniper wouldn't get a chance to shoot at them. We made it over all right. But we hurried, I tell you.

"Once we got past, we sat down for a 10-minute break. One man from another company decided he wanted to go to the toilet, so he walked away from the group into the trees. The sniper shot him and he died instantly."

Another time, Bailey was leading part of the battalion in one direction when he passed another group of soldiers about 100 to 200 yards away going in the opposite direction. "We thought they were Americans, they thought we were Japanese," Ryan recalls. The two groups exchanged waves and no shots were fired.

Chances are Bailey, the ex-basketball coach, might have called it a "no harm, no foul" contact.

On another occasion a sergeant was leading a small group on one of the trails when he turned and saw two Japanese stragglers marching in line. In the army, any army, it seems, a soldier automatically falls in if he sees a line.

The two Japanese were quickly removed, probably permanently, as Ryan recalls.

* * *

Eugene Frost had served with Bailey since New Guinea. He recalls an incident on Leyte when the battalion was preparing to move its base from atop Hill 1525:

"While waiting, Jap mortar fire killed one of our runners. Our men wrapped him in a poncho, dug a shallow grave, then buried him in the presence of our battalion's Catholic priest and myself.

"No words were spoken by the priest, which caused me to ask him why he had not prayed for the soldier. His answer was that all the priests and chaplains had agreed not to pray over any dead except those of their own faith.

"I reported what he said to Colonel Bailey. He quietly explained to the priest that in the future he was to pray over anyone who was killed, regardless of faith. His orders were clear. The priest did not have to call the pope or Billy Sunday for clarification."

When Eugene Frost was promoted to captain, he figured his odds of living through the war were better. That changed when Bailey confirmed a company commander in another battalion had been killed. "Yes," Bailey said, "even company commanders get killed."

In a short time, the 1st Battalion began an attack near the Limon-Ormoc road. Bailey and Frost were together, no more than two feet apart, when a Japanese mortar shell landed between them. "It just laid there, half buried in the ground, failing to explode. We looked at each other with a sickly kind of smile," Frost said.

A few days after that Frost remembers overhearing Bailey on the radio. "He was verbally crawling all over the division chief of staff, a full colonel, for not having sufficient supplies. He bluntly informed his superior as to the fix we were in and that the regiment had failed to respond to his requests. We soon received the food, ammo and whatever else Bailey had sought."

By the time the unit had reached the battalion objective, Frost had 19 men left in his company. "We were on the crest of a low ridge when Colonel Bailey sat down beside me. A Jap rifle bullet went down the side of my helmet and buried in my left shoulder. Colonel Bailey looked at me and smiled. There was no way I could even think about going back to the aid station until later that day when the remainder of the battalion was relieved."

* * *

Don Ryan and Lloyd Fish lost track of the dates, but eventually the battalion turned west toward the Ormoc Road, which was the main supply line for the Japanese forces in northern Leyte.

Fish refers to it as "a sorry road," single lane, carved out of the side of the ridges, rising steeply on one side, falling sharply down the other. Finger ridges ran down from the east to the west.

"We put in a road block at the end of one of the ridges overlooking the road, machine guns, bazookas and riflemen in place," Fish said. "The road was like a reverse 'C' with a finger ridge knoll at the top, a curve to the east, then the second knoll. Bailey's command post was further up the ridge to the east."

After the positions were established, Bailey told Fish, "Come on, we're going down the ridge to see how they're doing."

They arrived at the time some Japanese light tanks decided to run the road block in an attempt to move south toward Ormoc. Fish describes what happened then:

"Five or six tanks emerged from behind the first knoll, and immediately encountered fire from the battalion roadblock. The first tank was immobilized on the highway, and from then on it was a turkey shoot. Some of the tanks drove off the edge of the road and became bogged down, but continued firing."

Fish scrambled for cover under the fire of the enemy tanks. Officers, after all, were not usually armed with anti-tank weapons.

"I have no idea what Bailey did, but I think he was close by," Fish remembers. "When I finally looked up, there was lots of smoke, some fires and GIs running up and down the highway. The tanks were not firing any more and several were ablaze.

"A young soldier had come out of his position and with a rocket launcher had proceeded to neutralize each tank as he ran by."

That young officer was Private First Class Dirk Vlug, who would receive the Congressional Medal of Honor for his bravery that day.

Vlug was 29 at the time, a veteran who had been with the division since he joined the 126th Infantry at Camp Livingston, La., and had made the trek across the Owen Stanley range back in Papua. His courage that day on Leyte would be one of the most heroic exploits of the war.

A half-century later, Vlug is still hesitant to discuss his fete. Like most men of strength and character, he is reluctant to focus attention on himself. He is more likely to shift the conversation to another incident on Leyte when he captured a Japanese prisoner. "He (the prisoner) spoke good English and thanked me for a chocolate bar," Vlug recalls.

Vlug also remembers Colonel Bailey. "I knew him, but he was an officer and I was an enlisted man, so I didn't know him well. He was a soldier's officer and I liked him. He didn't have the normal Army protocol and he was no Chicken Henry. He came out of the ROTC . . . but he was a lot better officer than some of the regular Army officers."

Vlug's action set the stage for the successful conclusion of the 1st Battalion's mission.

* * *

Food sometimes was scarce during the Leyte campaign, field rations often the only meals available. When the 1st Battalion was en route toward Limon on the Japanese flank, the men went eight days without fresh food. It was a time when transport planes would not fly without fighter escorts. Those fighter planes, Don Ryan explained, were tied up in operations at Ormoc where the Japanese were landing reinforcements.

It was no wonder, then, that the men of the 1st Battalion were surprised to read later in the Stars & Stripes newspaper that all troops in the Philippines had been served turkey dinner for Thanksgiving.

"We didn't get our turkey dinner until around Christmas when the fighting on Leyte was over," Ryan remembers. "As a result, because we hadn't been getting much to eat, a lot of the troops wound up with dysentery."

Don Ryan would soon leave the 1st Battalion, having been named the regimental communications officer. Bailey's unit, thanks to Ryan's suggestion about the use of lighter weight wire, had been the only battalion that had any communications back to the regiment during the fighting on Leyte.

"I told Colonel Bailey that I didn't want to leave the 1st Battalion. I wanted to stay with him. He said, 'No, they need you back there. So I guess you'll have to go and straighten things out.'

"That placated me, I guess, so I went back. That was the last time I was with Colonel Bailey."

* * *

O. O. Dixon, who also was a battalion commander at the time, recalls an incident on Leyte that reveals more about Bailey, the officer:

"We had a regimental commander who had been sent over from the States. I think he had been an instructor in the Command General's Staff College and it was obvious he was not a field officer. He was not a leader, we'll put it that way. He was given a mission from the division commander to use two battalions to push down the Ormoc Trail."

One of the battalions was under Bailey's command, the other under a new commander who had just worked his way up to a major and was eager to succeed. Dixon adds:

"This colonel (the new regimental commander), believe it or not, issued his field order by pulling a manual out of his hip pocket. He delivered his order to the two battalion commanders based on five paragraphs he read from that manual."

When he finished, Dixon was told later, Bailey asked about the boundary between the two battalions because the map of the jungle the colonel unrolled showed no identifying features. To answer Bailey's question, the colonel drew a line across the jungle which not even a surveying crew could have found. "That," the regimental commander said, "is the boundary between the battalions."

The colonel then asked if there were any other questions.

Bailey had one. "We only have rations for the next day. When will we get a resupply of rations and ammunition?" The colonel replied, "Well the train will catch up with you. Just move on."

The other battalion commander did just that. Bailey, however, took his battalion about 200 to 300 yards into the jungle and sent word back that he was being held up. He wasn't about to move on until he received rations and ammunition for his men.

"That," Dixon says, "was characteristic of Bailey as a leader. It showed that he would not put his men in jeopardy, that he cared about his unit. When the ration and ammo train caught up he sent back word that he was no longer being delayed and proceeded forward."

The commander of the other battalion, not as combat-wise as Bailey, but eager to follow orders, sent out a platoon that was wiped out when it proceeded too far.

* * *

There were occasionally hours, even in combat, when men could relax. When those times came, the cribbage board, which Harry Richardson calls "a very important part of our meager baggage," came out. "We never made a move without it."

Once the card game started, Bailey, encouraged by Richardson, would begin his recitation of the Robert Service poetry.

It was Richardson who also remembered the rare times when the men were each issued two cans of beer. "We would wrap the cans in a towel with an insecticide bomb that was set to dispense Freon. We thought that was a unique refrigeration system."

Photo, courtesy of Harry Richardson
Lt. Col. Bailey drinks from "water cooler" in Philippines

Lloyd Fish also remembers those card games. "Bailey never missed an opportunity for a small-stakes poker game or a game of cribbage. These were somewhat non-ending games. When there was a lull in the combat action the games picked up where they left off. I was mostly a kibitzer as I never could play cards well, but I enjoyed watching and listening. The enthusiasm and fun of the moment were always contagious and the memory of the scene, a field desk or a rude table of bamboo covered by a poncho or blanket, candle or lantern light, the night sounds of the tropics, and the players' expressions of joy or disgust at the turn of the cards, I can still recall."

There was more, however, to Bailey than card games and merriment. "There was," Lloyd Fish recalls, "a very human side, which was obvious from his conversations and the photographs of his family he often displayed. It was evidence that he was deeply in love with his wife and very proud of the young son that he had never seen."

It was a comfort to Katherine Bailey and to his parents, Jim and Mamie, to know that no matter where he was or how occupied he was with the enemy, Cladie Bailey always remembered his family.

"We didn't have to talk to Colonel Bailey long before we felt like we knew his brothers and sisters and everyone in the family," one officer wrote to them later.

* * *

The battalion would continue to fight, its Company B keeping continuous pressure on the enemy position which seemed to be the last hold up of the advance on December 19, 1944.

On December 22, General Gill issued General Orders 104, Headquarters, 32nd Infantry Division:

"Today the Red Arrow (32nd) Division successfully completed its primary mission of forcing a passage through the mountains from Pinamapoon to the Ormoc Valley. After 36 days of the bitterest hand-to-hand fighting yet experienced in the war, the Division has annihilated the 1st Imperial Division and this determined action has shortened the completion of the Leyte Campaign.

"Every officer and every enlisted man in the Division as well as those attached played a vitally important part in the Division's success."

It was written that the Leyte Campaign appeared to have marked for the 32nd Division its emergence from a sometimes bewildered and often scattered group of units into "an integrated division capable of smooth team play."

Colonel Cladie Bailey, and scores of others, had helped make it that.

* * *

The division combat history is even more descriptive about the Leyte campaign:

"The combat troops and their equipment were water-soaked in the first downpour, and never completely dried from then until the division was relieved. Foot travel, even on level terrain, was laborious because of the heavy, sucking, clinging, knee-deep mud. The slopes and tops of mountain ridges were as boggy as the valleys, but the infantrymen slipped and slid and crawled forward. They slept and ate and fought in a sea of mud, while supply troops conquered the same tenacious footing to give them the wherewithal to continue. Nature and the enemy had done their best, but the 32nd could not be stopped."

* * *

Colonel Bailey had crossed the Owen Stanley Mountains, fought at Buna where he was wounded, led his battalion at Saidor and Aitape and helped drive the Japanese from Leyte. He had been in the South Pacific for three years, had been in combat almost continuously for a year. There would be, however, little time to rest. After a two-week recess from battle, the 126th Infantry Division would again be in action.

PART VIII

CHAPTER XXVIII
Villa Verde Trail

After that respite, the 32nd Division was again on the high seas, this time headed north to Luzon, a 500-mile long island where 110,000 combat-ready Japanese troops lay in wait. The enemy, desperate to slow the American advance, was certain to offer firm resistance.

Other American forces already had fought their way into the heart of Manila, but held only a fourth of the vital island. The 127th Infantry had advanced into San Nicolas and on to Santa Marie and the Cabalisian River, where the road ended and a razorback ridge rose steeply from the plain.

It was there the Villa Verde Trail wound sinuously over the 6,000-foot range, described in a division combat history as "clinging to the mountain sides, balancing on narrow knife-like ridges, plunging into steep valleys, only to climb again, twisting and turning to the next barren, wind-blown peak."

The attack along the Villa Verde, called "the fight for the bowl," lasted from February 12 to 24. It would be the 126th

Infantry Regiment's assignment to conduct a probe of the river valleys that would continue until April 3.

The days on the trail were still hot and the rains poured down as the dry season ended. The nights were cool and the familiar smell of pine trees scented the air as the division fought its way onto the knife-like ridges of the Caraballo Mountains. It was a welcome change from the jungle damp of Buna, Saidor, Aitape and Leyte.

There was, however, little change in the enemy's resistance. Its will to fight to the death seemed to increase as the war grew more and more hopeless for the Japanese.

Caves offered the Japanese strong defensive positions as the 126th Infantry advanced up the Ambayabang River valley below the Villa Verde Trail. The enemy at times took the offensive, making fanatic attacks on command posts, reserve units and artillery positions.

* * *

On Luzon, before the 1st Battalion engaged in heavy fighting, company kitchens were set up so men could fill their mess kits, eat what they wanted, then dispose of leftovers in garbage cans.

The civilian population, Captain Eugene Frost explains, faced a food shortage so severe that natives would gather at the garbage cans and ask for the uneaten food. The soldiers, of course, complied.

Regimental headquarters soon sent word that civilians no longer should be fed. "Colonel Bailey countermanded the orders from his superiors and we continued to feed the natives. We all agreed it was right to do so," Frost adds.

Bailey was a humanitarian as well as a soldier.

It was about that time, Frost recalls, that Bailey learned he had been offered a position as the regimental executive officer. "He said he was turning down the offer. He liked, he said, commanding a combat unit. And he said he felt that he might lose touch with the men and officers who were doing the fighting," Frost explained.

Lt. Col. Cladie Bailey outside tent on Villa Verde trail

—Photo, courtesy of Horace Carter
Captain Bailey in card game at Brisbane, Australia

—Photo, courtesy of Don Ryan
Sign reflects that even in combat there can be humor

—Photo, courtesy Harry Richardson

Cladie Bailey and Harry Richardson in New Guinea

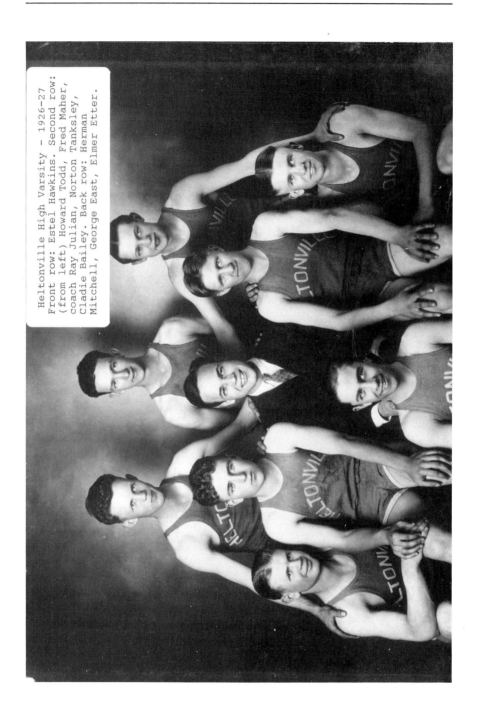

Heltonville High Varsity - 1926-27
Front row: Estel Hawkins. Second row:
(from left) Howard Todd, Fred Maher,
coach Ray Julian, Norton Tanksley,
Cladie Bailey. Back row: Herman
Mitchell, George East, Elmer Eter.

Heltonville High Varsity – 1927-28
Front: Estel Hawkins. Middle: Fred
Maher, coach Ray Julian, Howard Todd.
Back: Ed Cain, Herman Mitchell, Ray
Turpen, Cladie Bailey. Glenn Allen.

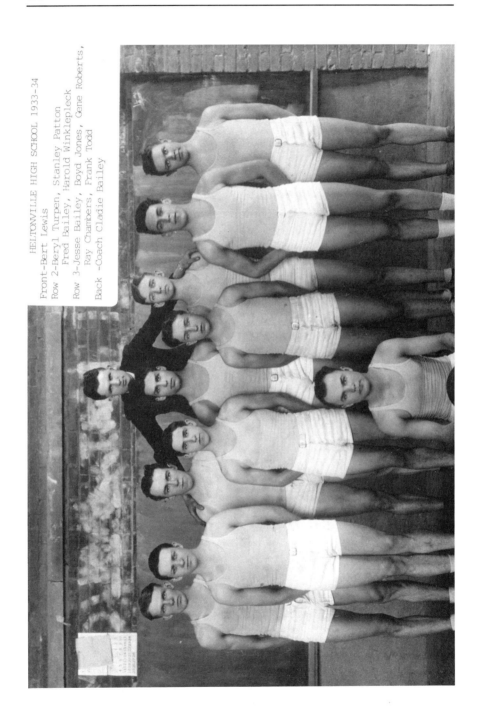

HELTONVILLE HIGH SCHOOL 1933-34
Front-Bert Lewis
Row 2-Beryl Turpen, Stanley Patton
     Fred Bailey, Harold Winklepleck
Row 3-Jesse Bailey, Boyd Jones, Gene Roberts,
     Ray Chambers, Frank Todd
Back -Coach Cladie Bailey

HELTONVILLE HIGH SCHOOL 1940-41
Row 1-Gerald Denniston, Robert Hillenburg,
      Coach Cladie Bailey, Ervan Murphy,
      Dale Norman
Row 2-Student Mgr Lester Neff, Opal Todd,
      Herman Chambers, Farry Todd, Dale Stultz,
      Doyle Lantz, Lorer Henderson
Row 3-Principal Loren Raines

—Photo, courtesy of Don Ryan
Services are conducted on Luzon for Lt. Col. Cladie Bailey

It was obvious Bailey wanted to be out front, out where the men were.

* * *

Lloyd Fish recalls the 1st Battalion's probing action up the Ambayabang River Valley north toward Baguio, then the division's drive up the Villa Verde Trail to the Cagayan Valley:

"The mountain range had herring-bone ridges nearly denuded of vegetation at the top with trees and brush in the valleys. From one standpoint it was good because we could see an aiming point from which to call for gun or air support; bad from another because the hills and ridges were infested with those cave emplacements."

It was in this area where General Yamashita had chosen to make his final defense of Luzon.

"I have no idea how many days we spent moving from one ridge to another, or even how far we moved," Fish relates.

"On the day I most remember, we were subject to infrequent, spasmodic mortar and light gun fire. The command post was in defilade, slightly below the top of the last ridge we had moved onto, but with no protection for the flanks as we were below the enemy held ridges."

Bailey, Fish adds, had the same accommodations we had, a fox hole with a poncho over it. "My fox hole was close to his, as were those of others of his staff."

(A day or two earlier, a Japanese round had landed in a bunker and killed the man who had been Don Ryan's communication chief.)

It was there that Colonel Bailey received a message from division headquarters that it needed an Assistant G-2, that Lloyd Fish was trained for the position and that it wanted him as soon as possible.

Fish remembers the moment. "Gus Bailey gave me a decision. 'Do you want to go now or tomorrow morning?' A ration/ammo party had arrived about that time, so I said, 'I'll go back with it, if it's OK with you.' He said, 'All right, take off.' So I geared up and left with the ration party."

It would be the last time Fish would see Bailey.

* * *

Meantime, Don Ryan, who was by then attached to regimental headquarters, heard a story that typified Bailey's sense of humor.

"A lieutenant colonel who had graduated from West Point had been assigned to take over one of the battalions. When he met Colonel Bailey, he remarked that he would give his right arm to have his reputation.

"I was told Bailey laughed, and said, 'Well, there are still a lot of Japs out there. You are welcome to go get them.' "

CHAPTER XXIX

Death in the Darkness

On March 26, 1945, Colonel O. O. Dixon, the friendly rival from back in Indiana, had became commander of the 126th Regiment and the man to whom Bailey thereafter would report.

By coincidence, the same day Lloyd Fish left the battalion, Colonel Bailey was ordered to move the unit across open ground to the base of a hill which was to be taken at dawn.

Before the move, however, Colonel Dixon arrived at Bailey's command post. Spotting him, Bailey razzed him, "What are you doing here? I thought you were the regimental commander. Regimental commanders are not supposed to be this far out."

It was the type of casual competitiveness the two men had continued since their high school years 18 years earlier.

Dixon replied, "If you remember, I was a battalion commander, too. I've been up this far before."

He explained that he had come to see if Bailey and his battalion were all set for their mission. Bailey replied that everything seemed to be in order.

* * *

That night, Colonel Bailey moved Company A of his battalion across the open space during darkness and deployed it into position to take the hill when morning came.

As he waited, he crawled down into a crater where a bomb had exploded earlier and went to sleep. His orderly, Tony Scuto, a young man who looked upon Bailey as a father figure, was nearby.

As they slept, the Japanese, on higher ground, rolled grenades down the hill into the crater. One exploded, killing Cladie Bailey, lieutenant colonel, U.S. Army, serial number 0296675. He had died out front with his men, up where the action was, not back in the relative safety of the battalion combat post.

He had been an example for his men and his officers and he had paid the price of freedom with his life. As Dirk Vlug, the Congressional Medal of Honor winner had said about Bailey, "He was no Chicken Little."

The date was April 20, 1945, four years and a day since he had reported for active duty. He had been overseas three years, had been in combat situations almost 500 days.

* * *

It was a week of tragic news. President Franklin Roosevelt had died eight days earlier on April 12 and Harry Truman had become commander-and-chief of U.S. military troops. Ernie Pyle, the noted war correspondent from Dana, another small Indiana town, was killed in the Pacific on April 18. Back home, the Bedford Times-Mail reported the deaths of two other Lawrence County men, Private John Root, 19, killed in Germany, and Corporal Daniel Roberts, 22, who also died on Luzon.

* * *

Lloyd Fish received the news of Bailey's death at regimental headquarters the next morning. "I didn't cry then, but as I write these words (in 1993), I cry now for a man whom I respected and admired, and for one who had so much potential, so much to offer as a husband, as a father and as a friend.

"I have always believed that Gus Bailey played a part in my continued existence by telling me to leave that evening. There is no way I can adequately express my gratitude for what he did for me. He put me on a career path, he sent me out of a combat situation where, if I had stayed, I may well have been killed."

Fish served 28 years in the Army. "I never found an officer I trusted or respected more than Gus Bailey. I have often speculated about how much he would have accomplished in life had he not been denied the opportunity," he adds.

* * *

Don Ryan had talked to Colonel Bailey over the phone the night before. He would later write in his recollections of the war:

"Bailey's promotion to commander turned out to be the best move in the world for our battalion. He was not only a fine, warm hearted individual but a terrific combat leader, respected by all who served under him as well as by his superiors. All the time I served with Gus, I never recall seeing him lose his cool."

* * *

Colonel Dixon received the word of Bailey's death the next morning. "I saw to it he (his body) was taken care of. I couldn't attend the services for him because I was so occupied at the regiment."

Dixon, who later became a career officer, said in a speech in the 1980s at a 32nd Division reunion:

"If I had to pick out one soldier in my regiment, the 126th Infantry, to typify a combat leader, it would be Cladie Bailey. I don't know of a single man in that unit that wouldn't follow if Bailey said let's march into fire. They knew he would march with them."

Bailey was more of a combat leader than a garrison officer. "He wasn't too anxious for everything to be ship shape," Dixon added.

It was that lack of "spit-and-polish, go-by-the-book" orders that endeared Bailey to his men.

* * *

James Hunt's return home to the States would be a bittersweet experience. He explains:

"I last saw Gus at his quarters on Luzon. He invited me to a poker game, which I remember because I had a fabulous hand, one which I could not take full advantage of because I had declared table stakes."

At that time, men had opportunities to return home under two different programs. Under one program, a priority point system based on number of months overseas, wounds, decoration and time in combat, men were allowed to take a leave which would permit them to go home for a few weeks, then return to combat.

Under a rotation plan, men could return home, then be reassigned in the States.

Hunt recalls that both he and Bailey were at the top of the priority list, but were not allowed rotation leave because the division general did not want to lose experienced combat leaders.

"Gus and I kept refusing leave, hoping for rotation. When our outfit went into Leyte, there were only three company grade officers who had started out together in Australia. The three were Gus, Erwin Nummer and me. Nummer was killed on Leyte, leaving Gus and me. On Luzon, Gus was offered a leave because he had a few more days in combat than I. He refused. I was so tired and weary that I decided to take that leave. The war ended in Europe while I was home and I never went back."

(It is believed Bailey declined the leave, knowing how difficult it would be to return to combat after a short time at home with his family. He wanted to remain with them, once he returned).

Hunt recalls, "Before I left Luzon, Gus asked me to call his wife when I arrived in the States and tell her he was doing fine. I called her from Camp Atterbury near Indianapolis. It was then I learned that he had been killed while I was en route home."

He adds, simply, sincerely, "Gus Bailey was a splendid officer and a good friend. I have three pictures from the war years on the wall of my den, all taken at Natunga on the north side of the Owen Stanley Mountains. One of those pictures is of Gus and his company officers."

* * *

Harry Richardson remembers that "Gus" kept a roster of officers of the regiment. "When they began to return home on rotation, he would strike them from his list. This made him feel closer to the time that he expected to return to his home and family."

He adds, "I am honored in so many ways to have known Gus. Time has not dimmed the memory of a great warrior and friend. We shall see him again!"

* * *

Eugene Frost had been wounded for the third time on the Villa Verde Trial and had not seen Colonel Bailey since. When he heard of Bailey's death he recalled that decision he had made to remain a battalion commander, rather than move to the safer haven of regimental headquarters. "I knew what he meant, but now, in retrospect, I wish he had taken that assignment as regimental executive officer when it had been offered to him a few weeks earlier."

The pictures of Frost's mind returned to those times when he would see Bailey in his tent, reading from a list that indicated when he might be rotated home. "He wanted to go home in the worst way, home to his wife and child. There was no officer in our division who deserved the chance to go home more than the colonel. Bailey, however, was not the cut of a man who would try to finagle his way out."

Frost adds: "Throughout all the fighting until his death, Colonel Bailey was an outstanding example of what battalion commanders should be. The men and officers in the battalion knew they were well led by the best."

* * *

Sol Jaffe would remember when Bailey issued orders to his staff and company commanders. "He would not stand over your shoulder or ask how you were doing. He would only expect to hear from his subordinate officers when they couldn't follow through on his commands. He was a memorable person I shall never forget."

* * *

Russell Gonsoulin had been rotated from Leyte back to the States where he heard of Bailey's death. "He was easy to get along with and he did not fuss at my mistakes," said Gonsoulin who still recalls Bailey's Hoosier accent.

* * *

William "Marty" Chapman was with Bailey's battalion on that night of April 19 and the morning of April 20. He would make the Army his career, serving 34 years on active and reserve duty.

Chapman saw Bailey's body when it was removed from the base of the hill, saw where a piece of shrapnel from the grenade had entered his chest, knew he had lost a friend and a leader. "Bailey was an outstanding officer. I served under many commanders in those 34 years. He was the best."

Company A succeeded in ousting the Japanese from the hill from which the grenade had come. But the death of Bailey had taken a toll on morale and esprit de corps.

Chapman tells what followed: "I never saw a battalion go to pieces as ours did the day the word spread that Colonel Bailey was dead. We were pulled out of the line for a few days because the battalion wasn't worth a hoot with Bailey gone. I think that if he had ordered us to march to hell, the whole battalion would have marched to hell. That's how much the men thought of him. He was a fine officer, a good tactician, and just a plain, regular sort of man everybody loved."

* * *

Horace Carter agrees that Bailey was highly regarded by his fellow officers. "He was reliable, trustworthy, sincere, and caring for his family and troops."

Carter remembers "Gus" as "a dry-witted Hoosier, a lot of fun. But he was not beyond standing up and expressing his opinions regardless of rank. He always saw to it that his men's needs were taken care of as best he could."

* * *

Elmer Geik, through Colonel Bailey's involvement, had been given a direct commission. He recalls that Bailey had volunteered the 1st Battalion to take the lead as it proceeded along the Villa Verde Trail in an operation that began on April 5.

He probably wanted to be out front, Geik explains, because he had confidence in his leadership abilities and the regimental commander was aware of his reputation for getting the job done.

He learned on the morning of April 20 that Bailey had been killed. The colonel's body was brought to Geik's aid station from where it was moved to a cemetery for burial.

"He did his part in every way," Geik relates. Geik too remembers the shock wave that went through the battalion when the news spread of Bailey's death. "A lot of the battalion officers were changed right after that. It was a rough time."

"He was an excellent officer. He was loved by his men," Geik still recalls, citing two examples:

* As a medic while an enlisted man, Geik often cut hair at the Army canteen in his spare time. When Geik became a staff sergeant, his captain ordered a stop to the barbering. Geik, however, resumed his practice when Bailey asked for a haircut and convinced the captain to change his mind. Geik would continue to cut hair until he received his commission.

* (Geik cautions that perhaps he shouldn't tell this story, then explains, "A lot of funny things happen in combat.") "Before the battalion started up the Villa Verde trail, Bailey decided to have a party for the officers. He sent one of the men over to the aid station to get a pint of GI alcohol for the poker players. I gave him a pint, which they must have mixed with some kind of juice from the rations.

"I never forgot that. It was the only time he ever sent for alcohol and I can still remember the look on that new medical officers' face when I poured that alcohol into the canteen. Anyhow, there wouldn't have been enough alcohol to do any harm to any of the men because most of the battalion officers were at the game."

Geik explains that chances are Bailey planned the party to ease any jitters the men may have had about the renewed action they would soon face.

Elmer Geik still laments his failure to write Colonel Bailey's relatives to tell them what a privilege it was to serve under him.

* * *

Bob Wray, who lived a mile from Bailey's home back in Indiana, was assigned at the time to a replacement depot on Luzon. When some men from the 32nd Division came to the depot in late April, Wray asked if they knew Colonel Bailey. It was then he learned of Bailey's death.

One of the men told Wray about an incident on New Guinea when the battalion was making a river crossing: "Colonel Bailey noticed some of the officers had gone to the rear. He stopped the entire unit until the other commanders came up to the front with him."

The news was a shock to Wray, who remembered those days back at Heltonville when he was a student and Bailey was a teacher.

* * *

Harry Richardson, "Gus' " closest friend, was chosen to command the honor guard at the funeral for Colonel Bailey in the Philippines. It was a dignified ceremony, one befitting an officer and a gentleman. The men with whom he had formed a mutual friendship were still out at the front and unable to attend the service. Bailey would have understood. The war was yet to be won.

A number of other officers and men agreed the battalion was not the same after Bailey's death. It had lost its leader, one who would not be easily replaced.

PART IX

CHAPTER XXX
A Time of Reflection

It would be almost a week after Colonel Bailey's death that the dreaded telegram would reach Katherine at her home on North I Street in Bedford, Ind.

"When you live more than three years on hope, you plan what you will do when the war is over," she would explain later. "When the telegram came, I thought at first it would say that Clade was home, that the words would be 'meet me.'"

He could, she explained, have come home that same month, but he would have had to go back in 30 days. "He said he couldn't do that, couldn't leave his wife and 'the little one,' after seeing us again."

Katherine, adds pensively, "I wished I had gotten a letter to him and told him to come on home and we could make every day seem like 10 years, even if he did have to return."

Katherine Bailey was a broken-hearted 22-year-old widow, facing an uncertain future as the mother of a three-year-old son. And now, she had to drive the 10 miles, out beyond Heltonville on Ind. 58, to tell Jim and Mamie Bailey their son had been killed in action.

The bitterness she felt would take a long time to heal. "He (Clade) had gone through so much and still didn't get to come home. It just didn't seem right, because so many others did get to come home who hadn't been gone nearly as long," she recalled, sadly.

* * *

The death of Colonel Bailey, "Cladie" to his parents, "Clade" to his friends at home, "Gus" to his compatriots in war, was reported in the Bedford Times-Mail on April 27, 1945.

A two-column headline in 36 point type reported:

Lt. Col. Cladie Bailey
Is Reported Killed In
Action On Luzon Island

The subhead read:

Former Heltonville
Basketball Coach
Held Distinguished
Service Cross

The text read:

"Lt. Col. Cladie Bailey, husband of Mrs. Katherine Bailey, 807 I Street, and son of Mr. and Mrs. James Bailey of Heltonville, was killed in action on Luzon Island in the Philippines on April 20, his wife was informed today in a message from the War Department.

"The War Department messages said a letter would follow.

"Colonel Bailey, who advanced rapidly in rank from first lieutenant to lieutenant colonel in less than four years, held the Distinguished Service Cross for extreme heroism near Buna on December 2, 1942, while serving as a lieutenant.

"The citation, presented while he was under treatment for wounds received December 19, 1942, in the New Guinea engagement, stated that as commander of a rifle company, he led an assault without regard for personal safety, inspiring his command by his example of initiative and courage.

"Colonel Bailey was a veteran of three years fighting in the Pacific. He was activated as a first lieutenant and inducted into the Army on April 19, 1941, at which time he was employed as coach of the Heltonville High School basketball team.

"He trained at Camp Livingston, La., Fort Benning, Ga., and Fort Devens, Mass. He sailed for overseas service in April, 1942, and had not been home since that time. He never had an opportunity to see his son, Cladie Alyn.

"Bailey was promoted from lieutenant to captain on December 31, 1942. He advanced to the rank of major on October 15, 1943, and was made a lieutenant colonel on May 15, 1944. In addition to the Distinguished Service Cross, he also held the Purple Heart.

"Colonel Bailey, who was 34, was a graduate of Heltonville High School and Indiana University in 1932. He was a member of the Heltonville High School faculty during 1933 and 1934, later becoming an officer in a Civilian Conservation Corps camp. He returned to Heltonville High School as coach of the basketball team in 1939.

"Survivors besides the wife, son and parents, are two sisters, Mrs. Doris Bowman of Heltonville, Mrs. Helen Dunlap of Redwood City, Calif., three brothers, James Bailey Jr. and William Bailey, both of Heltonville, and Jesse Bailey, with the U.S. Army in Germany."

* * *

Jesse, Cladie's brother, was in Germany, around Heidelberg, as he recalls, when he received a letter from home telling him his older brother had been killed.

"The ironic part came when I received a V-Mail letter from Clade three days later which he had written from Luzon. We had written each other about once a month."

Brother Bill recalls he was in Heltonville when he heard the news that Cladie had been killed. "Grant Mark (a Heltonville resident), who had been loafing at Stan Hanners' barbershop, saw me coming, met me out on the porch and told me. I don't know how he heard about it."

In small communities, news travels fast, even more so when it is about a home town hero.

* * *

On June 13, 1945, a headline in the Bedford newspaper, reported:

2 New Gold Stars
On Mundell Flag

The news story read:

"Two new gold stars were added to the Mundell Christian Church service flag Monday afternoon during funeral service held there for Corporal George E. Trogdon, husband of Mrs. Irene H. Trogdon of Terre Haute, and son of Mr. and Mrs. Wes Trogdon of the Mundell community, who died Monday June 4 at Camp McQuaide, Calif.

"He was injured in a vehicle accident at Watsonville, Calif., on Saturday, June 2, in which three other soldiers from Camp McQuaide received fatal injuries.

"Corporal Trogdon, and Lt. Col. Cladie Bailey, who was killed in action on Luzon Island in the Philippines on April 20, 1945, were the servicemen honored, the stars being placed on the flag by Corporal Charles Kapfer, who served as military escort in the return of Corporal Trogdon's body from California."

* * *

Colonel O. O. Dixon, upon returning from the Philippines would speak later at a service at Mundell Church, which Cladie Bailey had attended as a boy.

Dixon recalled that Bailey had enjoyed life as a teen-ager. "I guess we all did more or less. I will say this—and I made the comment at Mundell—that he had changed in his attitude toward life to the point that when the battalion would hold a religious service of any kind, Bailey would be there.

"One of his desires," Dixon told the congregation, "had been to get back and see his wife and his son."

* * *

The war for most Americans would end that August after the U.S. dropped the atomic bombs at Hiroshima and Nagasaki and forced the Japanese to surrender.

It would not be over for a long time for Katherine Bailey. It would be several months before she received the personal effects he had with him at the time of his death. Among those items was a small leather holder with a picture of Katherine and another of their son, Cladie Alyn.

The worst time for Katherine came when the husbands of her friends started coming home from overseas. Each arrival would be a reminder that Clade would not be back.

She would be comforted, however, in the years and months to come by Jim and Mamie and the other Baileys and by the words she heard from those who had known Cladie.

A friend named Hersh Bennett, for example, had received a V-Mail letter from Bailey, who had written that he wanted to get home. "I want to teach that son of mine how to play ball," Bailey told him. Bennett gave Katherine the letter and asked that she save it for Cladie Alyn.

Katherine was visited often by Walter "Dutch" Holt and his wife. "Dutch," who had played baseball with Bailey, once brought Cladie Alyn a large metal airplane, which was hard to find at the time.

"And the Baileys," Katherine said, "were just wonderful people. They always treated me, even after we knew Cladie wasn't ever coming back, as if I was one of them. They always treated me wonderfully. I have always been awfully proud and happy that I was in that family."

* * *

On May 12, 1946, Katherine attended a memorial service at Indiana University for Cladie and other I.U. graduates who had been killed in World War II.

A ceremony was held at Mundell Christian Church on December 7, 1947, six years after Pearl Harbor, when the flag bearing Bailey's gold star was removed.

EPILOGUE

It would be almost four years after his death that Cladie Bailey's body was returned to the United States in February, 1949.

"No matter how long it is you still want him back. I thought that was truly him," Katherine would say upon seeing the Army issued metal casket when it arrived, escorted by a lieutenant colonel.

A hearse from the Jones Funeral Home in Heltonville took the casket from the railroad station in Bedford to the Bailey home where it remained until services at Mundell Church.

The Baileys had a burial plot at Mundell Cemetery with room for four graves, one each for Mamie and Jim and two others. They asked Katherine, who had remarried in the meantime, if she would like Cladie buried there. "I thought if anything would happen to Cladie Alyn, it would be nice if he could have that spot next to his father," she explained.

Services were at 2 p.m. on February 26, 1949, a Saturday when another basketball season was ending. The Rev. Joseph Black, a boyhood friend of Jim, the father, and the Rev. Gene Dulin, who had been a student at Heltonville when Cladie taught there, conducted the funeral.

Pall bearers were Loren Henderson, Gerald Denniston, Lester Neff, Opal Todd, Harry Todd and Robert Hillenberg, all of whom had played for the coach. Honorary pall bearers were Clyde Sherrill, David Rach, Ervin Murphy, Doyle Lantz, Dale Stultz and Robert Wray, men who had been his students before they, too, went to war.

Sixteen nieces and cousins were needed to carry the floral tributes to the grave where American Legion members conducted memorial rites.

Gold Star mothers of Bedford and Heltonville attended the service in groups as did the American Legion auxiliary.

* * *

Katherine had married Forrest "Fade" Mathews in 1946, but she still remained close to the Baileys. "I know," she says, "that it hurt them when I remarried. But they insisted that we still visit them. Mamie would continue to visit me and my husband the same as she visited her other children.

"After Mrs. Bailey died (in 1954), Jim came about every fifth Sunday to spend the day at our house. He always had time to spend with Cladie Alyn. I recall once when Cladie was supposed to fix some moccasins for the Boy Scouts, but didn't. Grandpa Bailey came, sat under a tree and fixed those moccasins."

Doris, Cladie's oldest sister, and Katherine became good friends. "We happened to stop for a visit with Doris and Jasper (Bowman) on Cladie Alyn's first birthday. It would become a tradition." Mother and son, often in the company of other sisters-in-law and their children, would spend each birthday with the Bowmans until Cladie Alyn was 21 years old.

At family dinners with the Baileys, Cladie's brother, James, befriended Cladie Alyn, playing with him and helping feed him and his own son, J. Ed., while Katherine helped in the kitchen. "That made me feel good," Katherine recalls.

Another brother, Bill, who had a number of children of his own, always had time to play with Cladie Alyn, tell him stories, tease him gently and see that he had an enjoyable time.

"And Jesse. I'm just real pleased with how he accepted my husband Fade and made him feel he was part of the family, too. For example, Jesse and Louise wanted only family members— children, grandchildren, brothers and sisters—to attend their 50th wedding anniversary dinner. They called and said they wanted me and Fade to be there.

"That's just the way it always has been. It's like you are in the family and we're going to see to it that you feel welcome. It is hard to know your brother isn't living and that someone else has taken his place.

"Before I married Fade, I told him, 'I am not over Clade. I won't give up the Baileys and my mother, who lived with us at the time. And I have this little boy. I am a package deal.'

"He (Fade) has been very patient. And he was such a good father. He never even thought of Cladie Alyn as 'step' and, while Fade wasn't Cladie Alyn's real father, Cladie Alyn always called him Daddy."

Katherine and Fade Mathews would have two sons, Mark and Danny, who would be like full brothers to Cladie Alyn. It would be Mark who would note that his dad had accepted his mother's continued involvement with the Baileys. "My dad is a big man because he accepts that," he once told his mother.

Katherine Mathews still cherishes a cherry cabinet Jim gave her after Mamie's death. When she suggested he ask his children if they wanted it, he said he considered her one of them.

"I still have it 40 years later and I can visualize Mrs. Bailey using it."

* * *

Heltonville High School had been without a home basketball arena for seven years when a new gymnasium opened on December 20, 1949.

It was dedicated in memory of Cladie Bailey and presented to "present and future boys and girls of Pleasant Run Township."

The school's basketball team no longer would have to practice at Shawswick and play all its games on the road as it had done since the 1942 fire destroyed the gym where Bailey had coached.

Bailey would have been proud. The Blue Jackets defeated Tampico in that dedication game. In years to come, his nephews and great nephews would develop their games in that gym which had been dedicated in his memory.

* * *

A four-foot tall reddish granite tombstone marks the grave of Cladie Bailey in Mundell Cemetery, a half-mile south of the location of the old Fullen School he attended as a boy. Etched in the stone is:

BAILEY - Lt. Col. Cladie A.
126th Infantry, 1st Battalion
32nd Division
Born Oct. 26, 1910
Died April 20, 1945
Killed in action on Luzon.

A wreath is atop the monument. "I always try to keep flowers there," Katherine says. "Before Doris (Cladie's oldest sister) moved west I went to the cemetery with her. It's sad now going without her."

Cladie's mother Mamie (1883-1954), his father James (1881-1959) and brother Justice (1907-1914) are buried in the same plot at the well-maintained rural cemetery.

* * *

Cladie Alyn Bailey doesn't remember reading much about his father until he was in the seventh grade at Shawswick School, a member of the junior high basketball team.

"Someone wrote an article after our first game in which there was a paragraph about me being Cladie Bailey's son. That would have been about 1955.

"I really haven't been told too many stories about my dad. My mother would talk about him when I asked, tell me about his days at Indiana University, the fact he pitched baseball there and was in a fraternity.

"About the only time anyone else mentioned him was to tell me they remembered him and that he was a good athlete and a great guy.

"I never saw him, of course, so I never knew him. As far as the kind of person he was, the traits, the attitudes he had, I don't know if I carried on any of those or not."

Cladie Alyn still has the red and white wool "I" blanket his dad earned as a pitcher at Indiana and many of the pictures and records his mother gave him when he left home.

He was too young to remember lighting candles for men who had been killed in service at a Gold Star Mothers program at Heltonville when he was just three. Neither does he recall being with his mother at a ceremony at Fort Harrison in Indianapolis when a Silver Star was presented posthumously to his father.

He does recall attending the 1958 Veterans Day dedication of the Disabled American Veterans chapter at Bedford in his father's memory. "I don't recall anything specifically except that there was a parade."

It was at that ceremony when a letter was read from Colonel O. O. Dixon, who remained in the regular Army for 20 years. In the letter, Dixon called Cladie Bailey "a leader of men" and added: "His government presented him with its second highest decoration. His outstanding talent was recognized time after time under the most hazardous conditions of jungle warfare. He rendered his country an outstanding record of service to the cause of freedom and he paid the supreme sacrifice."

(On November 11, 1993, the Lt. Col. Cladie Bailey Chapter of the DAV organized its first Veterans Day observance.)

Colonel Cladie Bailey would never hear his son call him "Daddy." That would be what Cladie Alyn called Fade Mathews. "He is a great guy," Cladie Alyn says of Mathews. "He never treated me like a stepchild and we've always had a good relationship. To this day, when I see him, I call him Daddy."

Cladie Alyn, like his carpenter grandfather Jim, prefers to work with his hands. That's why he passed up an opportunity to attend college and works as a skilled employee for Cummins Diesel in Columbus.

Among his four children is a son named Cladie, who was born November 18, 1962. His other children are Traci Ann, born April 10, 1965, Sherri Lynn, born November 28, 1967, and Andrew Lee, born January 6, 1971.

* * *

Cladie Bailey's brother, James, was killed in a sawmill accident on July 22, 1970. Brothers Jesse and Bill still live at Heltonville. Sister Helen resides in Nevada, moving there from California. Doris Bowman, whose late husband Jasper worked as a carpenter with Jim, is now in a Bedford nursing home after spending several years with Helen in California.

* * *

Katherine and Fade Mathews' first son, Mark, is basketball coach at Bedford North Lawrence where his team won a sectional championship in his initial season in 1993-94.

He, too, was an outstanding basketball star at Shawswick High School. It was after one of his games at Shawswick that

Katherine would hear a poignant comment from Opal Todd, one of Cladie Bailey's players at Heltonville.

Todd stopped her and said, "The good Lord took Clade from us, but he gave us Mark." Katherine Mathews thought at the time, and still does, "How true that was."

By coincidence, Mark Mathews was an assistant coach when Bedford North Lawrence won the Indiana state basketball championship in 1990. The star of that team was Damon Bailey, a Hoosier legend who still holds the state scoring record. Damon, who later played at Indiana University, was a great nephew of Cladie Bailey.

Katherine's third son, Danny Mathews, is a painting contractor in Bedford.

She and Fade still live near Bedford. "Fade is very much a family man. He is quiet, not opinionated. He is a good man who has been good for me."

Katherine Mathews still hears from men like Harry Richardson, Don Ryan and O. O. Dixon, all of whom have visited with her over the years. She sent Richardson that Robert Service book of poems Cladie had memorized, thinking he might like to keep it. Instead, Richardson had a friend rebind it like new, then returned it to Katherine as a gift.

* * *

The high school at Heltonville closed in 1974 when county schools merged with Bedford to form Bedford North Lawrence. Grade school students still play in the gymnasium, but few are aware it was dedicated to Cladie Bailey.

* * *

O. O. Dixon, served 20 years in the Army, and later resumed his teaching career after a long recess from the classroom. He is now retired and lives in Indianapolis.

Francis Walden, who served as an enlisted man under Bailey, farms near his home town of Stinesville, Ind.

Harry Williams, who, like Walden also crossed the Owen Stanley Mountains, is still a New York Life Insurance agent in Chester, S. C.

Elmer Geik lives in St. Joseph, Mich. Sol Jaffe spends winters in Delray Beach, Fla. Horace Carter is in Rocky Mountain, N.C. Russell Gonsoulin resides in New Iberia, La., and Herbert Smith in Neillsville, Wis.

William "Marty" Chapman spent 34 years on active and reserve Army duty and now resides at East Harwich, Mass.

James Hunt, who was with Bailey from Camp Livingston to Luzon, is an attorney with Hunt, Moritz and Johnson in Lima, Ohio.

Don Ryan, who played a major role in research for this book, spends winters in Bradenton, Fla., and summers in Schenectady, N.Y.

Lloyd Fish, who provided colorful insight about Colonel Bailey, lives in Inverness, Fla.

Dirk Vlug, the Congressional Medal of Honor winner, resides in his hometown of Grand Rapids.

Eugene Frost, a company commander under Bailey on Luzon, lives in Roanoke, Va.

Tony Scuto, Colonel Bailey's aid who escaped serious injury when the grenade exploded in the bunker, could not be located.